THE WELCOME

The Welcome

BY

BABETTE DEUTSCH

WITH PICTURES BY

MARC SIMONT

HARPER & BROTHERS, PUBLISHERS
NEW YORK AND LONDON

THE WELCOME

Copyright, 1942, by Babette Deutsch
Printed in the United States of America

II - 2
THIRD EDITION
E-T

For

TRUDE FRANKL

ACKNOWLEDGMENT

THE words of the Ukranian folk song, "Yuletide," as translated by Jacob Robbins, are reprinted by permission of the publisher from the Botsford Collection of Folk Songs, vol. 2, copyright 1922, 1929, 1931, by G. Schirmer, Inc.

ILLUSTRATIONS

CHAPTER ONE

"Hi-ya, Thursty!"

Thursty, so called not because of his quenchless thirst for all-black sodas, but because Dwight Thurston, Jr. offers no better nickname, flung up his arm and wigwagged vigorously.

He hadn't wanted to go back to school. The summer behind him had been a grand one, with nothing to spoil it but having his small sister Cecilia, commonly known as "Silly," tag after him now and then. It was one thing to get up early for the sake of a swim before breakfast, and quite another to have to get up in order to take a nine o'clock math test. But now that he was climbing the old hill, and saw Peter and Richard waiting for him near the top, all the familiar sights and odors, from the burning brush pile near the playing field to the eraser that left a chalky smell when you threw it across the room, seemed to swarm toward him and offer welcome.

"Hullo, you ole debbil, you," cried Thursty, pulling the cap off Pete's crisp black hair and poking the lanky Richard in the ribs.

"Hullo yourself," they answered, neither of them a match for the bulky Thursty, who looked like the blue-eyed ruddy-cheeked son of a Viking and sometimes went berserk like one.

The three boys thumped each other on the back and marched slowly forward, arms linked, the sturdy figure of Thursty between shambling sandy-haired Richard and spry, swarthy little Pete. As they approached the spacious stone building, over which the flag tossed brightly in the autumn wind, Richard asked, wrinkling his forehead:

"Who've we got for class teacher this year, anyway?"

"Andrews, you dope," said Thursty. Everybody knew you had Andrews in Second Form.

"Is he O.K.?" asked Richard.

"Sure, he's all right," said Pete. "Teaches shop. Shows you how to make some really decent things too. Sometimes he umpires basketball. He's awfully tall."

"You think so 'cause you're a runt," objected Thursty. "He's no Paul Bunyan."

"Well, neither are you," from Peter.

"All I want to know is, does he crack down on you if you're late or something," Richard asked anxiously.

"You planning to be late or something?" Thursty said teasingly.

"It's easy enough for you, Thursty, living up here just a couple of blocks from the school," answered Richard. "But I bet if you lived down in Manhattan and had to take the subway up to the end of the line every morning, you wouldn't always make your nine o'clock either."

"Aw, you're nuts, Richy," said Pete scornfully. "I take the subway up here too, don't I? What about most of the fellows? They don't live round the corner from school. I'd rather have to take the subway any day than be buried up here away from everything. Gosh, Thursty, I don't see how you stand it an hour's ride from a decent movie."

"I like it fine," asserted Thursty. "I'm getting a beaut of a kodak for my birthday and I'm going to fix up a swell dark-room. I'd have the heck of a time doing that in a New York apartment. Know what, fellows?" he asked, proudly. "I was born in our house thirteen years ago next Saturday, and so was my father and so was his father."

"You going to put up a name plate, Thursty? THIS IS THE BIRTHPLACE OF DWIGHT THURSTON JR. BORN THE SAME DAY AS HIS FATHER AND HIS GRANDFATHER?" asked Pete, his black eyes sparkling.

And then they were at the school entrance, with a dozen boys to pound on the back and a scattering of old teachers to shake polite hands with. Before you could say "knife" it was time to find the classroom and get their new locker keys and listen to the old story about beginning the year well by coming on time and doing your homework and not fooling in the washroom and staying home when you had a bad cold because it might really be scarlet fever or mumps, and the school didn't want any avoidable quarantine.

Thursty had heard it all before. He sat with his arms folded across his chest, and a listening look, but he kept stealing glances about the room to see if all the old boys were back, and guessing what the line-up would be for the teams. He was a good soccer player and at football his square bulk could nearly always block a drive. Thursty rather prided himself on his shop work too: Andrews would find him O.K. there. Only, he thought, with a twinge of foreboding, he was apt to get in dutch in the classroom: things sometimes ganged up on him, and he would begin to feel like a young bull with a red rag in front of him, and then there was no holding him, and that meant all kinds of trouble. It was different with the others: Pete always managed to slip out of a tight place by sheer slyness, and Richard was such a quiet guy that the teachers never landed on him hard.

Thursty straightened up and looked Andrews square in the eye. He was a tall, lean, agreeably ugly young man. Thursty, staring at him with a kind of urgent innocence, thought he glimpsed a twinkle in the gray eyes under the unruly mop of hair, but was not sure enough to grin back.

He looked away hastily and turning, caught sight of a boy he had never seen before. Thursty sized him up. He wasn't particularly tall, though he was thin, and there was no more down on his upper lip than on that of Jim Clark, the biggest boy in Second Form. But though the stranger appeared to be no older than the others, he looked different somehow.

Nearly every year there were one or two newcomers, some of them scholarship pupils, as Thursty guessed this boy might be. Only last term there had been Booker T. W. Jones, the gangling warm-eyed colored boy across the aisle. Richard, whose mother had been born in Richmond, hadn't wanted to sit next to him at first. They had called him "Alphabet Soup" because of his long name, and thought no better of him because he was immensely polite and had a voice that the music teacher praised. But he had turned out all right — made the basketball team and come out first in the broad jump on Field Day. Besides, he didn't really like singing: it was just a foolish idea of his family's.

Thursty glanced from Booker to the stranger, looked back at Booker, and winked. Booker winked back. He was one of them now, and resented strangers with the rest. And there was something odd about this new boy, with his tobacco-colored hair cropped short and the solemn gray-blue eyes.

"Well, boys," Andrews was winding up at last, "I've spoken my little piece. Some of you have been in the school long enough to know it by heart. Some of you never heard it before. I hope you'll all remember it just the same. In a moment you can do the talking. But first I have to make sure you're all here."

He had been striding up and down in front of the class, but now he halted, ran his hand through his untidy hair, and sauntering over to the desk took up the little black book from which he called the roll. Seeing Andrews' eyes fixed on the book, Thursty gingerly lifted his desk lid, drew out a sheet of paper and a broad elastic and proceeded to roll the paper into wads and manufacture spit balls with which to tell off each member of the class as he answered to his name.

"James Clark," said Andrews.

Jim Clark was tall and sat in the back of the room, so it was not an easy matter for Thursty to snipe him, but he managed.

"Here," said Jim with a faint gasp, and an I'll-get-you-for-this glance about him.

"Peter Davis," said Andrews.

"Here," shrilled Pete, who sat near enough to respond to Thursty's shot with a quiet kick on the shin.

"Richard Evans."

"Here," mumbled Rich, stifling a grunt as Thursty hit the mark, and throwing him a reproachful look.

"Booker T. W. Jones."

"Heah." Booker, forewarned, grinned broadly and bounced Thursty's missile back at him with a ruler.

Thursty grinned in reply and waited for Andrews to call the next name.

"Ernst Keller."

The new boy straightened up and answered, "Here." Thursty took accurate aim. The spitball landed neatly and stingingly in Ernst Keller's face.

He cried out, surprised, looking about for his assailant, his pale face flushing.

Thursty was disgusted with him. Nobody made a fuss about a spitball. If you didn't like it, you hit back, silently, like Pete.

Andrews had put down the roll book and come forward, his eyes raking the class.

"I'm sorry, Ernst," he said in his quiet drawl. "There seems to be some fellow here who left his manners in the locker room. You mustn't think we're all so rude. It's no affair of mine," Andrews went on, not looking at the new boy now, but glancing from one member of the class to another, "if you want to greet your old friends with missiles, that is," — he rubbed his jaw — "as long as you don't consider me one of your old friends. But I do mind," he said more sharply, "when you behave that way toward a newcomer. He's apt to think you're a set of savages. I know you're not: you're just ordinary boys," — did Thursty imagine that Andrews dwelt on the "ordinary"? — "and I hope Ernst will soon find out that you can be quite a decent lot. I don't know which one of you ought to stand up and apologize, but whoever it is, I suggest that he do it not with words but with actions. Class is dismissed for gym."

Ernst looked about for his assailant

"Old Preachy-Teachy," muttered Thursty, hot-faced, as he hurried to catch up with Pete and Rich.

The locker room smelled as usual of wet boards, sweaty shirts, rubber matting and soap. But the three did not race as usual to see which would be first in his gym togs. They had to talk things over.

"If there's any apologizing to be done," grunted Thursty, pulling off his shirt, "that guy ought to apologize to me. Getting me a lecture the first hour with his squealing!"

"Andrews didn't know it was you," said Pete. "You're all right. Where d'you s'pose he comes from, this Ernst Keller, I mean?"

"He talks like a German," whispered Richy.

"Whatever he is, I don't like him," said Thursty. "Gee, fellows, hurry, it's late!"

Ernst's behavior in the gym didn't help him particularly. He was pale and skinny and it looked as if he would be of small help to any team. When they scrambled for the showers afterwards he would easily have been pushed into the last place, but Booker, with the courtesy that the boys had learned to forgive him for the sake of his rougher virtues, stepped out to give Ernst a chance.

"Sank you — I mean, thank you," said Ernst, carefully correcting his outlandish accent. "Rreally I didn't mind it when you hit me viss zat — with that — what-d'you-call-it? I just didn't know it was coming."

"Spitball," answered Booker, grinning, "but I didn't do it."

"Oh. I thought because you were so kind . . ."

Thursty poked his dripping head out of the shower curtains.

"It was me," he said.

"Oh," said Ernst. "So."

Thursty had been almost ready to say he was sorry, but the foreignness of Ernst's response annoyed him, and he was silent.

The stranger was forgotten during the classes that followed the gym period. When lunch hour came, and Thursty maneuvered to be at the same table with the other members of the bunch, he was solidly content. It was good to sit hunched over his plate in the wide noisy dining hall gobbling with the rest and gabbling between mouthfuls: good to complain in the old way about the large amount of carrots and the small amount of gravy: good to discover that he was heavier than the lot of them: and to sneak two helpings of dessert, though it was only a miserable rice pudding with raisin sauce.

After lunch the class assembled to hear about the general project for the year. Even that Thursty looked forward to, as part of the familiar pattern. The Second Form, Andrews told them, was going to explore the United States, at least as well as this could be done in a school that stayed put on the upper tip of Manhattan Island. The boys would be paired off for various jobs. And since two of them were clever with pencil and brush, they would be assigned to do a map of the States, with pictures of American heroes scattered over it. They could pick any notable figures they chose, real or imaginary, from Johnny Appleseed to Zachariah Taylor, but they had to paint in somebody for every section. It was plain to the class that one of the boys on this job would be Dwight Thurston, for Thursty seemed to have inherited the skill of his

Uncle Tom, who actually had his pictures bought by museums while he was still alive. There was nothing sissy about Uncle Tom either: he did his stuff up near the North Pole and down on the volcanic islands off the South Seas. He'd come to the school once to talk about his adventures. Nobody was surprised when Andrews said:

"You're one of the map makers, Thursty." (It was a count for Andrews that there was no stuffed-shirtiness about the way he addressed the boys). But then he added:

"And your side-kick will be Ernst Keller, here."

That dope! Thursty said to himself, looking miserably to Pete for consolation and getting only a malicious wink in reply. The one comfort he had was that Ernst would probably go home on the same subway train with Pete and Rich and that they would haze him properly. They'd teach a guy to squeal, thought Thursty. My side-kick! thought Thursty. Well, painting together would provide its opportunities, too: a brush full of water color could drip in the most unexpected places.

"Rrrevenge is sweet!" Thursty reminded himself cheerfully at the end of the day, as he trotted toward home. But his gloating imagination of vengeance was tinctured unpleasantly with the knowledge that he would have to give a fairly full report at the dinner table of what the first day in Second Form had been like. He wouldn't mention the incident of the spitball, of course. But he'd have to say something about this Ernst Keller, and he was sure Pop and Moth' wouldn't see eye to eye with him about the fellow.

He was about to go round to the back door in the hope of sweetening his homecoming with a piece of cake from Delia's

rough generous hand, but the front door stood open. Moth'
was in the hall, not even seeing him, and — why, that was
Dr. Hendricks! Gee, thought Thursty, hope he didn't come
to give me an injection or something. He was about to retire
and sneak round to the back when his mother called,

"Dwight!" And then, turning to the doctor with an ex-
asperated laugh: "What shall we do with Dwight?"

"Well," murmured Dr. Hendricks reflectively in an
astonishingly small voice. He was an enormous man with
small blue eyes twinkling from under a tall white forehead,
great ruddy jowls, two chins, and a paunch that looked
as if he fed exclusively on the things he said were not good
for growing boys. "Well," he repeated, "the safest thing
to do is to ship Dwight — yes," he rubbed his second chin,
"ship Dwight off where he can't catch it."

"His Granny's!" exclaimed Moth'. "Of course. Then he
won't be anywhere near Cecilia."

"What's wrong with Silly?" It would be awful, thought
Thursty, if Silly had gone and caught something and he'd
have to stay down in Manhattan for the duration. What was
the use of a house where you could fix up a darkroom for your
new kodak that had been promised for your birthday, if
you couldn't stay there to get your birthday present!

"Silly, you call her?" Dr. Hendricks laughed wheezily.
"Well, she was silly enough to get — we don't know what,
but we think maybe it's going to be measles. Anyway, we're
keeping you clear of it, young man."

"You mean I can't even go up to my own room?" asked
Thursty.

"I mean your mother'll pack up some things for you in

a jiffy, and I'll drive you over to the subway so you can get to your grandmother's for dinner. How's that?"

"That's awful!" "Lovely!" said Thursty and his mother in one breath.

"I thought so," wheezed Dr. Hendricks with a chuckle, and gave Thursty a gentle shove toward his car.

CHAPTER TWO

Going down on the southbound subway, with one of Pop's old suitcases tucked importantly between his knees, Thursty was at once disgruntled and pleased. It was rather a relief not to have to explain at home about Ernst Keller. Moth' and Pop wouldn't understand the dislike he'd taken to the fellow. And of course Granny would prepare a royal reception for him. He sometimes felt that Sarah, the large colored woman who bossed Granny about the way Delia bossed Moth', thought even more of him than Delia did: Sarah hadn't known him when he was a baby, which was an advantage, and she didn't play favorites with Silly, either. Living at Granny's, he'd be traveling up to school and back with Pete and Rich, which was all to the good. And he might get to see some of the exciting things that Pete boasted Manhattan was full of: a bank holdup, maybe, or some big guy like Joe Di Maggio walking into a cigar store.

What if he'd have to have his birthday at Granny's? That wouldn't be so hot. He'd get his kodak all right, he was certain of that, but he couldn't fix up any darkroom, and if Granny gave him a party they'd have to be careful not to hurt any of her precious old knickknacks. If he didn't have a party, it would be kind of dull and unbirthdayish. And all along he'd been looking forward to this birthday as something very special. He'd had a strange hunch that something exciting or at any rate unusual would happen that day that he couldn't even imagine.

He came back with a thud to Silly's measles. The problem wasn't his birthday celebration. The problem was where would he sleep. Granny, being a Manhattanite, lived in an apartment, with a kitchen so little you couldn't go in while Sarah was there fixing things. Thursty sighed heavily. There wasn't a spare bedroom: he'd be put on one of the couches in the living room, and have to get up for an awfully early breakfast. He probably couldn't read in bed, and there'd be sure to be trouble about listening to his favorite radio programs.

He looked down disconsolately at the floor of the train and caught sight of the suitcase. It was plastered with torn labels: Hotel Adlon, Berlin. Victoria Palace Hotel, Paris. Grand Hotel, Geneva. It was a very old suitcase. Thursty began imagining that he was a hunted spy, disguised as a refugee. But it wasn't much fun because there was nobody to pretend with him. He began plucking off the labels, and then the guard came through and said crossly:

"Whuttar ye doon littherin up the flure av the train wid yure dirrty bits av pay-purr! Tis the loikes av you make all the thrubble in the worruld." Which Thursty didn't believe, although Delia sometimes said much the same thing in much the same way.

At last he reached the station nearest Granny's. Up the subway stairs, and down the street he went, the suitcase banging against his legs.

"You muss be awful hongry," said Sarah understandingly as she opened the door to him. And at once Granny, supporting her long lean lame old body with a stick — Pop called it her Big Stick — hobbled forth, crying out in her creaky voice:

"Well, Dwight, I'm delighted that you're here. And how is poor little Cecilia?"

"Oh, I guess Silly's all right," said Thursty.

"Now why do you call her that? It's such a silly name!" said Granny, not intending the pun, which made Thursty laugh more than if she had.

"Now go and wash up, Dwight, and Sarah'll give you something to eat. I don't dine at this hour, but she'll take care of you."

"O.K.," Thursty suppressed a grunt. It was horrid being called "Dwight" all the time as though he were his own father. And there was something so stuffy about Granny's apartment, with its heavy furniture and its tables full of delicate ornaments and silver-framed family pictures, that he didn't know how he was going to stand it.

The old girl meant well enough. There was broiled chicken flanked by a golden-brown waffle for dinner, and not too many green peas, and the dessert was a baked apple in a red glaze of crusty sugar with a plate of Sarah's almond-sprinkled cookies beside it. After dinner Granny paused in directing Sarah how to make up the couch for him to ask if there wasn't a radio program he wanted to listen in on.

But Thursty couldn't help feeling strange. He had to remember not to splash in the bathroom, which was full of all sorts of funny jars and bottles, and he took ever so long falling asleep in that great long room, crowded with curious pieces, with the shadows falling in mysterious patches on the rug, and the shriek and grind and rumble of the city coming in through the open window.

When he woke in the morning he didn't know where he was until he saw Sarah at the far end of the room setting the table for breakfast in ponderous silence. He waited till she'd gone back to the kitchen before he leapt out of bed and down the hall to the bathroom, dragging his clothes after him. It seemed awfully queer, washing and dressing in there, without having Silly bang at the door to let her in, or Moth' call him to hurry. Breakfast was a lonely affair, for Granny didn't rise so early. Thursty was glad he was quit of Silly's nonsense and the fuss over making her eat her egg. But it was funny, all right, eating all by himself in the great crowded room. He gulped his milk, stuffed a crust of toast with a lump of jam on it into his mouth, and jumped up.

It was queer again, leaving the house, with Sarah standing patiently in the doorway while he waited for the elevator, instead of Silly waving to him from the window. He wondered how long measles lasted. In his place, a kid like Silly would be homesick.

Trotting down the street toward the subway, Thursty recalled that Pete and Rich always got into the first car of the train. Wouldn't they be surprised to see him again if they were on the train he caught! He'd make it sound great, being on his own as it were. He wouldn't let Pete or Richard know there was any part of it that he minded.

The train was pulling into the station as Thursty pushed through the turnstile. He passed rapidly through to the first car. The only passengers were a couple of laborers and a thin scattering of boys on their way up to school, but none who

He waited till she'd gone back to the
kitchen before he leapt out of bed

were in his class. The heck with it, thought Thursty. What was the good of Silly's having measles if this was all it got him?

"Good morning!"

The hesitant voice, the throaty "r" in "morning" seemed at once odd and familiar. Thursty turned to see Ernst Keller settling in the empty seat beside him.

"Oh, hello," answered Thursty indifferently. "Seen any of the fellows?"

Ernst shook his head.

There was an awkward pause. It occurred to Thursty that perhaps Ernst preferred not meeting Pete or Rich: they must have hazed him pretty thoroughly last night on the way home. Finally Ernst spoke again:

"I thought you lived near the school."

"Yep, I do," said Thursty, "but my sister's sick and they're afraid I'll catch it, so I'm staying at my grandmother's till she's O.K. again."

"I do not stay with my sister, either," volunteered Ernst.

"What's the matter? She got the measles too?"

"No. It's just that — she is living with friends of my —" Ernst seemed to have some difficulty with his speech: "— of my father's. And I am living with Susi."

"Oh," said Thursty, not able to figure it out. Perhaps Ernst's mother had divorced his father because she'd discovered he was a Nazi. But then what was Ernst?

"It is tough," Ernst offered, the American phrase sounding foreign as he said it, "to be away from your sister."

"You joking?" asked Thursty.

"No! I have never been away from Erica before. Except for three minutes." Ernst smiled faintly: "I was born three minutes before she was — you see, we are twins."

"I guess that's different," admitted Thursty. " 'Course, Silly's only a baby, not more'n six. She's cute enough," he had to defend Silly before a stranger and a foreigner, "but she bothers a lot."

"Yes," said Ernst, "even Erica sometimes — after all, she is only a girl. But I can't say that to her. She gets wild."

"Yep," Thursty mumbled. He wasn't interested in Erica. "Golly," he said, talking rather to himself than to Ernst, "it's funny coming home and not being able to go into your own room!"

"Yes," Ernst answered, his voice lifted as though he were about to go on, but he did not.

"You going to say something?" asked Thursty.

"No, nossing," said Ernst, uncomfortably.

"What were you going to say?" Thursty insisted.

"I mean, it is funny, like you said, in a bad way: funny."

"What do you know about it?" Thursty asked wonderingly.

"I know," said Ernst, and then stopped abruptly, as though he wished he had not spoken.

"What d' you mean?"

"Well, when — when Erica and I came home from school that day . . ." Ernst stopped again.

"What day?" Thursty prompted him.

"When the Storm Troopers had been there."

"Go on," said Thursty, big-eyed.

But Ernst did not go on.

"What did you do?" asked Thursty at last. Golly, that was something. It sounded like a movie.

"I don't remember exactly. They took my father away. My mother got sick. So Erica and I had to go to England. We stayed there about a year. And then we came here."

"Oh," said Thursty, and was silent. He tried to reconstruct what he had just heard and fit it into the picture he had formed of the boy beside him and his twin sister Erica. But it was too hard. And then there was the mysterious Susi with whom Ernst was living, while his sister stayed elsewhere.

"What did your father do?" asked Thursty. Maybe it was wrong to ask, but when a fellow told you that much, you had to know more.

"Pappi?" Ernst flushed and corrected himself: "My father? He was a biologist."

"No, but I mean, what did he do that they — took him away?"

"Nothing. He was a socialist."

"So's my father!" said Thursty, astonished. "Only," he added severely, "he wants us to lick the boots off the Germans." Some of the talk Thursty had heard across the dinner table at home had given him the impression that there were 57 varieties of socialists, including some fake ones like the Nazis, who were poison to the real kind.

Ernst smiled. And Thursty grinned at him briefly. It was funny, their fathers thinking alike. In class, when they had straw ballots, Pete voted Republican and Richard voted

Democrat. It bothered Thursty a bit, but he forgot about it as soon as elections were over. Last time he'd worn three Roosevelt buttons, a Willkie button and two Thomas buttons. Thursty wondered what it would be like, going to jail for wearing a certain button. He was glad when they got to school and he could shake Ernst Keller, and the uncomfortable thoughts he started.

And there were Pete and Rich not even knowing that he was living in Manhattan too now!

The first chance he got, Thursty boasted to them about being alone at his grandmother's, with nobody but the old lady and Sarah to look after him. He'd really be looking after *them,* if anything happened, he guessed. He half hoped something would happen. That reminded him of Ernst's story. He told the boys about it, and about Ernst's twin sister Erica. But when Pete asked who Susi was, and why Ernst was staying with her, while Erica stopped with other people, he couldn't answer. It was all very puzzling.

"There's something queer about him," Richard insisted.

It wasn't just his accent, or, as Pete, a noticing boy, pointed out after lunch, his way of carefully loading his fork with a little bit of meat and potato and vegetable at each mouthful instead of just eating like everybody else. There was more to it than that.

Up in the art room afterwards, sketching out the map of the States that the pair of them were to stud with figures of great Americans, Thursty was convinced of Ernst's foreignness.

"Andrews said we could paint in anybody we thought

was great, whether he was real or not," Thursty reminded Ernst, "so long as he was an American. Now Paul Bunyan, he'd be in the West . . ."

"I thought Bunyan was an Englishman," Ernst interrupted, "and went on a pilgrimage."

Thursty stared. To confuse the giant lumberjack with the author of *Pilgrim's Progress* was a bit thick. But when Ernst admitted that he thought Babe Ruth was just a kind of candy, and didn't see that they had to include the Lone Ranger, Thursty was ready to give up.

"If y'ask me," said Thursty, "the Lone Ranger's greater than a lot of presidents, and all the vice-presidents, and he's as American as — as Thanksgiving."

But Ernst knew nothing about Thanksgiving!

Thursty was telling Pete and Rich about it on the way downhill after school, when Ernst came along.

"How is your sister today?" Ernst asked.

"O.K., I guess," said Thursty. What business was it of Ernst's, anyway? he thought. Besides, he didn't know. "My mother'll tell me tonight when she phones," he said, and with a backhand gesture managed to knock Ernst's cap off.

Pete caught it on the fly and threw it to Richard. Ernst didn't seem to get the joke. As they ran down the hill, throwing the cap back and forth, he leapt awkwardly after them like a young goat. Once the cap fell on the edge of a puddle and got mud on the visor.

"S-sursty!" he cried out, "please — zat is my one hat!"

"Sursty!" Pete mocked, "zat is his one hat, give it back to him, zat's a good boy!"

"Thursty!" Ernst pleaded, articulating carefully: "please!"

They had reached the subway stairs. It would be fun to race into the train, with the cap as a trophy, leaving Ernst behind. They wouldn't hurt it any, they'd take it back to school tomorrow, but he'd learn not to be so fussy about his one hat, which was really a cap. How many hats did he think *they* had?

Thursty, clutching the cap, made a dash, with Pete and Rich hot on his heels, and Ernst panting after. The doors of the outgoing train slid closed just as they reached the platform, and the train pulled out. Too late. They'd all have to wait for the next one.

"I don't mind," Ernst gasped, "only Susi gave it to me and she will be so sorry."

"You mean she'll be so sore," Thursty corrected him.

Ernst shook his head, with a funny little smile.

"Who is Susi, anyway — your nurse?" asked Pete.

"She is my best friend," said Ernst.

"Oh, go on, give him back his cap, Thursty. You don't want to hurt his girl friend's feelings," said Pete.

"Sure," Thursty threw the cap to Ernst.

"Sank you, I mean: thank you," he murmured, catching it and stuffing it hastily into his pocket. Maybe he thought they'd snatch it again if he wore it.

As they entered the train and slumped down on the seats, Thursty decided that they had teased Ernst enough for one while. Riding down, the talk was about the next day's game and how soon Andrews would think they were ripe for an exam.

Richard left the train first, and then Peter's station came. Thursty, left alone with Ernst, did not know what to say.

It was Ernst who spoke first: "It is not nice — going to a strange house to sleep."

How the heck, Thursty asked himself, did he know what I was thinking?

"It's not too bad at Granny's," he answered.

They were pulling into the station as another train pulled out, and in the clamor all Thursty caught of Ernst's remark was the word, "Welcome."

"What?" he asked.

"Oh, that's where Susi — I'm sorry, I must go!" and Ernst hopped out of the door just before it banged shut.

What's this mystery about Susi anyway? Thursty wondered. He was still puzzling about her, and about the welcome Ernst had so oddly extended, when he reached Granny's house. Maybe Susi was a spy, who hid her nef — what was that word? — nefrious? — her something practices behind a boy's back.

CHAPTER THREE

"Dwight, is that you?" Granny called sharply. "My! Aren't you late?"

"Yeah. Nope." Thursty answered the questions in order. Golly, was there going to be an Inquisition every night when he came home? Tomorrow afternoon there'd be a game at school, and he'd be much later than this!

" 'Lo, Granny." He swung into the room where she sat frowning over her knitting, dropped his schoolbag with a thud and wished he could tear out to Delia's kitchen for a glass of milk and a handful of cookies.

"Hello, dear. You'd better wash up right away. And then get your mother on the phone. I want to know how Cecilia is. They weren't sure when I called at noon."

Maybe, thought Thursty hopefully, as he tramped into the bathroom, Silly had given them a false alarm, and old Doc Hendricks would say he could go home tomorrow. That would be swell. Specially with his birthday coming.

Moth's voice sounded cheerful enough as it came over the wires. He could almost see her standing at the 'phone, patting her shining hair that was slightly mussed, her blue eyes alight with the special smile she had for him — and for Silly, too, he admitted without enthusiasm.

She wanted to know how he was, and whether he'd had a good day at school, and if there was anything in particular that he wanted from home. Thursty's heart dropped into his heels at that question. It could mean only one thing: he'd have to stick it out at Granny's.

25

"Silly's not very sick," said Moth', as though that made it all right. "But it does look like measles, and you'll have to stay away until it's safe for you here."

"Golly, Mother, but how long'll that be?"

"Two weeks perhaps, three at the most. Try not to make extra work for Sarah, and we'll have a party to welcome you back. It's funny, but Silly seems to miss you. I guess she's so used to your teasing that she can't do without it!" Thursty could hear the little laugh in Moth's voice, but it didn't make things any easier. "Buck up, Dwight!" she said then more firmly. "We'll try to see that you have a good birthday, even if you can't be at home for it. Be a good fellow, and don't let Granny give you too many sweets! Better put her on the wire. Good-by, darling."

" 'By," said Thursty, bucking up obediently with a sour grin. "Hey, Granny, Moth' wants you."

Thursty was gnawing the end of his chop bone before Granny finished talking. She came hobbling in, and sat down at the table with him.

"Well, Dwight," she said, "it looks as though you'd be celebrating your birthday right here."

"O. K.," muttered Thursty, thinking that he'd like to have Rich and Pete and the rest, but even with Sarah's spicy sandwiches and lavish chocolate cake to make the day interesting, what, at Granny's, could they *do*?

He comforted himself with the reflection that he'd have a chance to talk things over with Moth' on the telephone beforehand: perhaps she'd have an inspiration. At any rate, the boys wouldn't be bothered by Silly wanting to tag along. He didn't know why, but there seemed to be something special about his birthday this year. If he'd been superstitious, he'd have imagined that it had to do with being thirteen. But it wasn't that at all. He felt as if something extraordinary was bound to happen that day, he didn't know if it would be good or bad.

Next morning the prospect of the first game of the season pushed everything else out of Thursty's head. The game would be only a trial balloon, but it might show if there was any Varsity stuff in the class. In any case, it was good to talk over the relative weight and leg-power of the fellows, to wonder what new stunts Coach Doyle had thought up, and to look forward to a hot dog with plenty of mustard down at Cohen's Soda Shoppe afterwards.

School seemed duller than usual, with the long wait for the end of the day, and nothing was duller than the face of Ernst Keller when the fellows talked about the chances for the eleven.

"But I sought — I thought that on the team there were only nine," he put in once.

"That's a baseball team, fella, don't you know the difference?" asked Pete.

"Difference between —" Ernst paused on the question.

"Baseball and football, you dope," said Thursty. " 'Course you can play with a smaller team, but that's only practice games and don't count."

Ernst shook his head over the mystery. Thursty groaned.

At last they were buckled into their togs and squatting out on the field, listening to Doyle's instructions.

"This isn't anything more than a tryout," he reminded them. "I know most of you fellows, and you can't have forgotten everything you learned last year even if you spent the whole summer fishing, which I bet you didn't. You're playing the First Formers this afternoon. But don't think it's going to be a walk-away for you. There's good material in the First Form this year. I see some new faces here too. What's *your* name?" Coach Doyle nodded to Ernst.

"Ernst Keller, sir."

"Well, Keller, you're pretty long in the legs. Guess you'll make a good end man."

"Yes, sir," said Ernst quietly, flushing.

"Now . . ." Coach Doyle delivered the usual brief pep talk, assigned the place of quarterback to Jim Clark and left it to him to line up the team and rehearse the signals.

Thursty, as he had expected, was left guard. As he had not expected, he was up against an enormous First Former whom he privately christened the Baby Ox. He didn't know they grew them so big. The boy looked as if he weighed 150 pounds. But if Thursty, for all his square bulk, was not as heavy as his opponent, he was quicker. A change of signals brought him the husky Booker's help in keeping Baby Ox within bounds. By the end of the first half the score was still 0-0. Play had been fast and hard. It was going to be just too bad if they couldn't lick those First Formers. What had happened to their quarterback? And Peter, who was short, but could move like greased lightning?

"Now listen, you fellows." It was Jim Clark. The impartial impenetrable Coach Doyle was lecturing the First Form team, and it was up to Clark to whip the Second Formers into real action. Thursty listened. Sure, he knew what the signals meant. Sure, he'd keep up his interference. But what about making a touchdown? What about scoring a couple of points?

"Doyle thinks we're going to take it lying down," said Jim, "and give the First Formers swelled heads just because they're new. We're not. We're going to beat those kids. And we're going to do it in a big way. The first game's just practice. Maybe!" Jim grinned scornfully. "We can't do a Statue of Liberty play — they'd catch on to that. But we can use a fake kick. Now you there," he nodded at Ernst: "You ought to be good at the leg-work. When the signal comes, it'll look as though I were getting the ball, but instead it's going to you. And it's your job to RUN."

There was barely time for a second swift rehearsal of signals when the whistle blew. They lined up. Thursty felt fine. Jim knew how to put it all over those babies, and over Coach Doyle, too, who secretly wanted the First Formers to win, or at least break even, so they'd feel they had something. Or maybe he was just testing the Second Formers, to see what they could do on their own.

Thursty's eyes, under a forehead pricking with heat, were glued to the ball. Almost before he could blink it was in play. The second half went well from the start. Richy made a leap and a miraculous one-handed catch of a swift pass.

But the First Formers weren't slow either. The wind was in their favor. They had put in a new halfback who was a whiz at bucking the line. Before Thursty knew it they had made a touchback. But there was still a chance if the Second Formers made a touchdown. Thursty figured that there couldn't be more than five minutes left to play, perhaps less.

Suddenly he heard Jim Clark shout: "7-7!" It was the signal for the fake kick.

Jim stood there looking as if he were ready to deal out a swift one. The First Formers swarmed about him to spoil the kick. But in obedience to his shouted command, the ball was sent spinning in the other direction toward Ernst Keller.

And Keller fumbled it.

Dimly Thursty heard the groans of the Second Formers on the side lines, the whistles and cheers of the opposing team's backers. Three seconds later the whistle blew. The game was over. The First Formers had won. And it was all Ernst's fault.

Thursty found himself beside Ernst as they tumbled into the locker room.

"If you hadn't of fumbled that ball, we might of made it. D'you know that, guy?" he asked.

"But," Ernst looked at him wonderingly, "I didn't know zat he was going to srow it to me zen!"

"Didn't know he was going to 'srow' it to you!" Thursty mimicked angrily. "Didn't he shout the signal? Didn't he explain we were going to get the best of 'em by a fake kick? Golly!" he groaned. "Guess you'll make a good *end* man — guess you'll *finish* us, that's what!" he punned dismally.

Ernst looked puzzled and ashamed all at once. Thursty, who had almost pitied him a moment ago for losing the game for them, had no sympathy to spare now.

The boys were always in a terrific hurry to get dressed and get out. Gym was never accepted as an excuse for leaving the building late, and besides, the overheated dressing room was a good place to leave behind. It was only the rush that kept

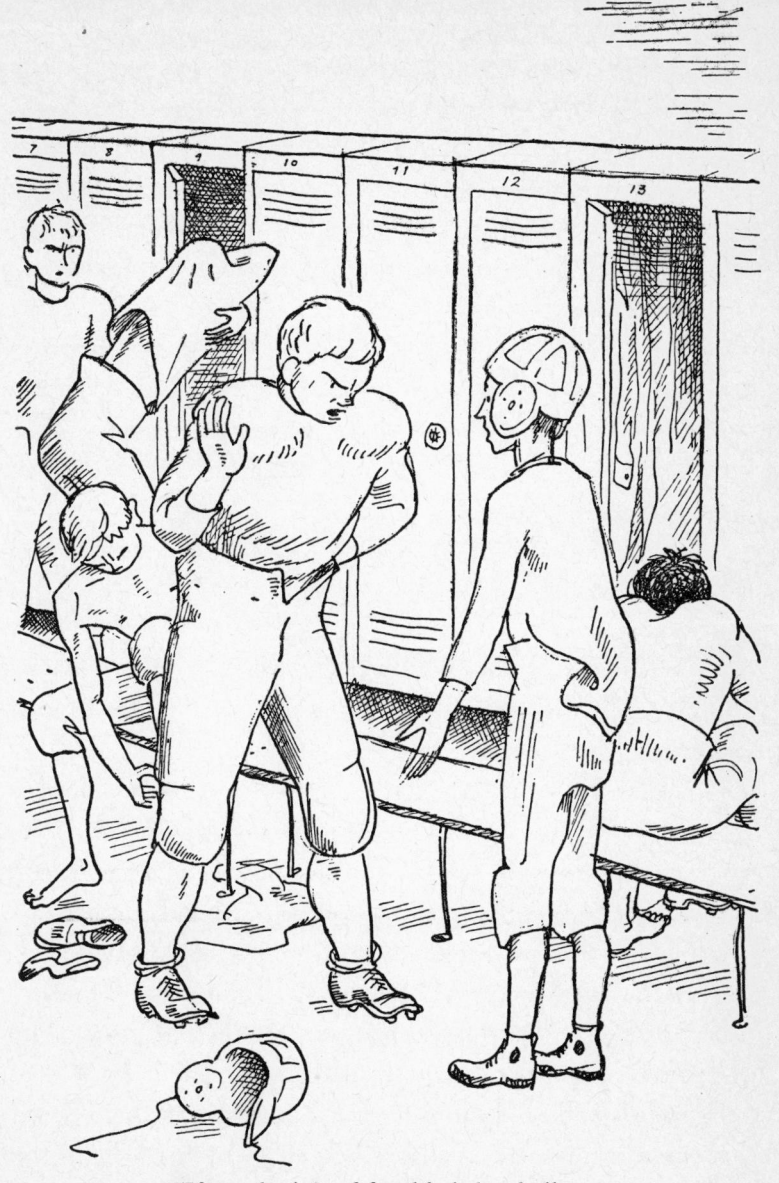

"If you hadn't of fumbled that ball, we
might of made it."

Thursty from entering into a furious discussion about the way Ernst had muffed his chance. It was the rush that was responsible for the fact that someone had taken Ernst's pants and then, when he found out his mistake, thrown them down any old place, so that Ernst couldn't find them till the bell rang.

Perched on the high stool at Cohen's Soda Shoppe, at the bottom of the hill, with an all-black before him and a hamburger sizzling on the griddle, Thursty might have felt better. But he didn't. Not even Richy's mention of his birthday cheered him. It was going to be terrible.

"Golly," he muttered, plunging his spoon into the glass so that some of the chocolate slopped over, "I don't know what it'll be like. I s'pose Granny'll let me ask the fellows, but I don't know what I'm inviting 'em *to*. It'll be — it'll be like a hot dog without mustard," he wound up disconsolately.

Richy laughed.

"Well, you'll get your kodak all right. So that's not so bad. Maybe you can even get some color films."

"And take a black-and-blue picture of Ernst Keller's eye with it?" asked Thursty grimly, gulping a mouthful of ice cream.

"What's the matter with the guy? Anybody can fumble a ball," said Richard soothingly.

"He didn't just muff it," explained Thursty. "*He thought Jim was going to make the kick*. He might have been a First Former for all he understood about our signals."

"The heck he did!" said Richy.

Pete whistled incredulously.

Their scorn of Ernst was comfort and joy to Thursty.

"D'you think he's a Nazi?" asked Richard eagerly.

"No. He's not," said Thursty. "I know that, because he told me about his father when we went up to school together. I told you. His old man got put in prison for being against the Nazis, and his mother got sick, and then he and his sister were sent to live in England, and now they're here. But there's something queer somewhere. Because his sister's one place and he's another."

"Aw, gee, Thursty," said Richard, "so's Silly in one place, and you're in another. That needn't be his fault."

"Well, *his* sister, her name's Erica, hasn't got the measles. And then there's this Susi person. There's something fishy about her."

Richard and Peter got out before Thursty did, so that he was left to ponder the problem alone between one station and the next.

Back in Granny's apartment, with Sarah hovering thickly in the background, putting the final touches to the table where he must eat his solitary dinner, Thursty forgot Ernst and Erica and Susi and the game and his birthday. He was occupied with trying not to look too wistfully at the radio, because Granny could not bear "Here's Morgan" or "The Lone Ranger" or "Superman" or anything really funny or agreeably bloodcurdling.

"Cheer up, Dwight," she said, almost as though she wanted to make up for her lack of taste in radio programs. "I have a surprise for you."

"Can I go home?" asked Thursty eagerly.

"No," said Granny in a sharp voice, looking hurt. "But," she went on, kindly, "your mother has arranged all about your birthday. I'm taking you to Radio City, you and your friends. Then there'll be no difficulty about upsetting things here. And you can all have a good time. I hope," she added, with a slight edge to her tone. She was still a little cross about Thursty's anxiety to leave her.

"That's swell," he said, trying to put enough enthusiasm into his voice to make up for his disappointment at having to stay on.

"But how'd Moth' know who to ask? Besides Pete and Rich, that is."

"Why, I think she said she called up Mr. What's'is-name — your class teacher — and got a list of the boys, so none of them would be left out."

"You mean you're taking the whole class?"

"That's right!" said Granny, triumphantly.

"Golly!"

There would be an awful crowd, but it would be fun. The lot of them in the theater together. It would be like Thursty's own show. Maybe that was why he'd had a premonition about its being a special day.

"And your mother said he particularly wanted her not to omit to ask the new boy — now, what is *his* name? I forget so easily. Eric? Edward?"

"Ernst," muttered Thursty. "Ernst Keller." Was he never to be quit of the fellow?

"Come on, boy, yo dinnah's ready," announced Sarah.

"Yes," Granny continued, hobbling after Thursty to keep him company at the table. "It's quite a story."

"I'll say it is," Thursty admitted.

"Oh, you know then?" said Granny, and went on explaining just the same, in the useless way old people did: "It seems Edward — Ernst, I mean, and his sister came over here on the invitation of some old friend of their father's. He and his wife were going to give both children a home. But when it came right down to it, they took only the girl, and so Ernst had to stay elsewhere. It's hard on him, because he's so attached to his sister, they're twins, your mother said. Now you, Dwight," and Granny's voice sharpened again, "haven't even asked how Cecilia is."

The heck with it, Granny seemed to think Ernst was nicer than her own grandson!

"How is Silly?" asked Thursty sullenly.

"A little better today."

Thursty refrained from asking if that meant he could go home sooner, and stuffed a fat shrimp into his mouth. It was a big juicy shrimp, doused with deliciously sharp cocktail sauce. Sarah was a grand cook. But Ernst was right about it not being nice at somebody else's house, even Granny's. Thursty didn't want Ernst to be right. He didn't want to invite him: he'd be a wet blanket on the party.

But the whole class at Radio City together! Thursty took another shrimp. Maybe it wouldn't be so bad at that.

CHAPTER FOUR

It was still dark that Saturday morning when Thursty woke up. As usual, it took him a little while to realize where he was. But he didn't have the usual smothered feeling, as though he were being choked by the heavy drapes and fine lace scarves that were part of the old-fashioned elegance of Granny's living room. Instead, he felt a tingling excitement.

He sat up and tried to see what time it was on the grand-father's clock in the far corner, but the face was too dim. He snuggled back under the covers. Not having to chase out of bed — he had to get up much earlier on school days at Gran-ny's than at home — contributed to his pleasure.

This, he thought luxuriously, was one of those special days. Christmas was one, of course, with its secrecy and ex-pectancy, its mixed smell of balsam and snow and spices, its glory of color: gay blue and red globes, shining gilt and crys-tal, floors pleasantly strewn with crisp paper, excelsior and bright scraps of ribbon, its marvelous foods: crackling roast goose and plum pudding wrapped in blue flame. And then, just as special, there was Fourth of July, with that early morning freshness you knew wouldn't last past dawn, and the delicious sharp powder smell that kept coming back all day, and the packets of tiny firecrackers that you started off with, like the coils of a red baby dragon, and the snap of the torpedoes, and then the endless, endless waiting, when even the giant crackers were all exploded, and the cap pistol ex-hausted, and there wasn't any more lemonade — waiting for it to get dark enough for the real celebration, and the disappointment when the first pinwheels didn't go off, and the gasps and whistles of delight as one after another the big pieces broke against the black sky in a shower of colored sparks like flowers on fire. There was Thanksgiving, too. And there was his birthday.

You couldn't help waking up too early on any of those days. On Christmas Day you got up and groped for your stocking, delightfully heavy and lumpy in the dark, and were busy with the contents until the rest of the family was awake enough for the day really to begin. On the Fourth you stole out before it was light and roused everybody with a minor explosion. Only Moth' objected that it scared Silly. And yet Silly, holding her ears, was the one to beg him to set off another. And on your birthday, well, that didn't have the particular fragrances and fun of the other occasions, or the expected quality of weather, or the hot rich foods that went with the one or the long, cold sweets that went with the other, but — well, it was good because you darn well didn't know what might happen. And for days now Thursty had been feeling in his bones that almost anything might.

Finally, when he couldn't stand it any longer, he got up and very quietly, so that Granny wouldn't be disturbed, dragged his clothes into the bathroom, washed in a hurry, and got dressed. He had to have the electric light on, to see what he was doing, and he spent a good deal of time in front of the mirror, feeling his upper lip and his cheek, wondering if he could possibly ask for a razor for his *next* birthday. After all, he was in his teens now. By the time he came out into the living room again, there was Sarah, setting the table for his breakfast, and a good smell of griddle cakes and frying country sausages: Moth' must have told them what his birthday breakfast should be. And then Sarah, her teeth very big and white in her broad brown face, was chuckling:

"Good mawnin', boy. An' may yuh have the happiess buthday evah!"

Before he could touch the small pile at his plate or the particularly interesting package on the floor, Granny came to the door of the living room, leaning on her cane with one knobby lace-covered hand and holding out a slip of paper in the other.

"Happy birthday, dear!" she cried in her creaky voice.

The paper was an envelope with two crisp bills in it — Granny explained that her real present was the party for the whole class: But the two dollars, said Thursty gratefully, would come in mighty handy for films or stuff, for that big package must be the kodak. He submitted briefly to Granny's tissue-soft kiss which smelt of violet water and peppermint, and tore back to the table.

Carefully, tenderly, greedily, he undid the wrappings.

O joy! O glory! That *was* a kodak! Never was leather such a sleek glossy black, never metal so keenly shiny. Thursty examined every detail, gloating. The lens, which was — yes, it was: f 3.5. And the shutter speed, which went up to three hundredths of a second. That meant he could take skiing pictures in the full glare of the snow, and sailing pictures with the sun ablaze on the water. And there were thirty-six snaps to one roll of film.

"Golly! Lookit!" cried Thursty. "A built-in range finder! And an exposure meter!" He hadn't any words. Suddenly he seized Sarah around the waist — it was like holding a warm, breathing barrel — and danced her down the room, while Granny gave little shrieks of anxious protest and amusement.

"O frabjous day, calloo, callay!" Thursty chortled. It was what Moth' exclaimed whenever she was feeling really jolly.

Thursty could scarcely do justice to the spicy little sausages and the homemade quince jelly for admiring the kodak. And then he was called to the telephone. There was even mail addressed to him. Not just advertisements of the National Geographic and requests to buy Defense Stamps, but real letters, or at least birthday cards.

And right after breakfast he took a picture of Granny, sitting very straight, with her hands folded knobbily in her lap, and a picture of Sarah, standing with folded arms, all curves. Before he knew it, it was lunch time, not that he was truly hungry, but he managed a chicken sandwich and some pineapple sherbet. And then the bell began ringing, and ringing again, and then soon the boys were filling up the room. Thursty was just beginning to feel that the whole class was twice as big and three times as noisy as he remembered it, and wondering if they wouldn't be late for the show, when the bell rang once more, and there was Ernst. For once Thursty was glad to see him. That meant they could go.

But he had reckoned without Granny. First she made Thursty count noses to make sure the boys were all there. And then she insisted on Sarah's seeing that everything with a key to it was carefully locked, and she tucked the keys in a little purse in a big old-fashioned bag which she stuffed with her knitting and stuck in the drawer of the big living room table. And then, when they were all set, she remembered that she had left the tickets in one of the bureau drawers, and they had to fetch the bag and pull out the knitting, slowly, so as not to unravel it, and dig out the purse and get the key, and unlock the drawer and find the tickets, and count them, and then lock up again, and put the key in the purse and the purse in the bag and the knitting on top . . .

If it hadn't been for the fun of showing off his kodak, Thursty would have wished that Granny had never invited the class at all.

But finally they were out of the house, and those that couldn't crowd into the taxi with Granny were herded toward the subway by Sarah, to meet the others in the lobby of the theater. And it was all jolly again.

It was a really exciting movie, and Thursty worked it so that he sat between Rich and Pete, and every time the villain came on they hissed in chorus. There wasn't much love-making, for which Thursty was grateful, and only one sort of sticky embrace which lasted so long that Pete yelled: "Time," and the usher came down the aisles sh-shushing, but everybody else laughed, and Granny was sitting too far away to know who had caused the disturbance. . . . There was a bright Disney short, and some neat close-ups of a ball game. It couldn't have been better if Thursty had arranged it himself. Afterwards they went across the street to a restaurant and there was a long table with a big sign — RESERVED — on it, and as they came in, the head waiter hurried forward and helped Granny down the room, whipping the sign off the table with one hand and pulling out her chair with the other.

"Everything all right, Madame?"

Granny nodded, and the head waiter bowed, waving the boys to their seats. But then he frowned faintly and bent over Granny's chair, to say something Thursty couldn't catch.

"See here," Granny quavered in an indignant whisper, "that boy is my guest, and Sarah is the best friend an old woman ever had. You ought to be ashamed of yourself!"

The head waiter bowed again, looking explosive and polite at the same time.

"Come here, Booker," cried Granny, "and sit right beside me. And Sarah, you see that they behave themselves at the other end of the table. Trying to Jim-Crow me!" Granny whispered furiously. She noticed Thursty staring, and gave a little push.

Thursty grinned. Granny was good when her dander was up. Had that waiter objected to Booker and Sarah because they were colored? Golly, it looked like it! It made Thursty mad to think about it. But he was relieved that, for all her rage, Granny hadn't spoken loud enough to be overheard. Their party attracted enough attention without that.

He felt better when they set before him a mound of multi-flavored ice cream in the shape of a kodak. The other boys had ice-cream footballs and ice-cream radios and ice-cream ukeleles. It was great. He had just finished the pistachio flash-bulb (that was one thing that was missing on his real kodak, thought Thursty) when they brought in a regular birthday cake with fourteen candles — one to grow on — that made everybody in the restaurant turn round to look and smile. Thursty felt uncomfortable but important.

"Make your wish, Dwight!" Granny called to him down the table.

Hastily wishing that Silly would get well quickly so that he could go home again, he took a deep breath, and blew.

It was a wasted wish, because of course Silly would get well soon and he'd go home. But he didn't mind. The cake was splendid. Jim Clark had two helpings. And they all ate the icing last, except Sarah, who ate it first.

"They's two kinds of people," explained Sarah: "the kind that eats his icin' fuhst an' the kind that eats his icin' last. Now I figguh maybe if somethin' happens, I won't git a chance to eat the icin' 'tall. Bettah have it straight off." And she did.

Nothing did happen to interrupt her, however, except that just as they were finishing, Pop came in, on his way back from the office, to wish his son a happy birthday in person, he said. For a gleeful moment Thursty imagined that Silly must be all right again and that Pop was going to take him home. But he wasn't. Thursty had to go back with Granny and Sarah.

As he plumped himself down on the little front seat in the taxi, taking care to mind Granny's knees, he had a let-down feeling. All along he'd been looking forward to his birthday as something very special. And now it was over. The movie had turned into just another movie. The ice cream and cake were eaten. And there was the disagreeable memory of that unpleasant head waiter.

It was over now, thought Thursty, as they drew up to the door of the apartment house, all but going upstairs and looking at his kodak again. It would have been better than any party if he could just have stayed home and fixed up his darkroom and taken some good shots and started developing. It was just like Silly to spoil it all.

Granny was ever so long finding her door key and giving it to Sarah, so she could let them in.

"You go ahead, Dwight," said Granny in a tired voice, "and turn on the light."

Thursty pushed the button in the foyer and Granny sat there to rest a moment while he went to snap on a lamp in the living room.

"Golly!" he shouted.

"What is it, Dwight?" Granny asked creakily.

Thursty didn't answer. After that first shout of bleak astonishment he could only stare dumbly at the wrecked room. What had happened? Who had been there? Someone who had had the laugh on all Granny's precautions. Every table swept bare of her precious curios, the piano looking naked without its rich scarf and the silver-framed picture of Moth', all the rest of the silver gone, too. . . . Thursty dashed into Granny's bedroom and switched on the light. The bureau drawers were pulled out, gaping, foaming with oddments. The closet door was flung wide, showing the interior half empty. Suddenly Thursty remembered. The kodak!

"Golly!" he half sobbed. It was gone, of course. You couldn't expect them to leave anything you cared about as much as that. Though you might think Granny's furs and old lace, her ivories and silver and jewels, would satisfy the greediest thief.

"Mah Lawd!" It was Sarah.

"What is it?" Granny called again testily from the foyer.

Sarah told her.

Granny gave a shrill cry. But at once she got shakily to her feet and began hobbling about, poking angrily at things with her cane, and crying that the radio was to blame. It took Thursty a few minutes to discover that in Granny's opinion it was the dreadful mysteries which he relished so much that taught thieves and murderers how to improve their talents. Thursty might have laughed, but he was too miserable over the loss of his kodak.

And yet, in spite of the stolen kodak, there was something thrilling about it. Deep down Thursty asked himself: Could this be what was to happen on my birthday? Could this be the exciting thing I felt in my bones was coming? Maybe, he thought, I have second sight. But then he thought: maybe I haven't or I'd have taken my kodak along with me.

He was disappointed when Granny said she would report the burglary to the police, and go to bed. She was quite worn out. Tomorrow they would see.

Thursty had to go to bed, too. But he couldn't fall asleep in the doubly disordered strange room. If only Silly hadn't got the measles, and he'd have been at home, his kodak would have been safe! The world, he thought, was full of horrid people, like whoever it was gave Silly the measles, and Dr. Hendricks who had sent him here, and the thieves who had taken his prize birthday present. Golly, how the place looked! He'd never seen anything like it before.

The curtain blew in the wind. It wasn't thieves, Thursty reassured himself, it was murderers who returned to the scene of their crime.

Anyway, he told himself, watching the curtain, this would

be something to tell the fellows at school. It would be better than any radio mystery. He could just see their faces — Pete and Rich and Booker and the rest. And Ernst? He wondered what Ernst would say.

Thursty rolled over and gave his pillow a thump. Ernst might spoil his burglary story, having that wonderful story about the Storm Troopers himself, and all those awful things happening to him. Of course, it wasn't exactly Ernst's fault, thought Thursty, but the burglary would have seemed more thrilling and terrible if he hadn't known about all that.

He rolled over again to the other side of the narrow couch. It was funny, he thought, but, sore as the guy made him, Ernst would be the only fellow in the whole crowd who would really know how it felt to come home to a crazy room and find the thing you cared about most taken away, perhaps for good.

Golly, they'd have to get his kodak back, whatever else stayed stolen. They'd just have to!

CHAPTER FIVE

The click of the camera woke Thursty. And then he realized that it wasn't the camera that he had just heard, but the flap of the shade against the windowpane. He had been dreaming. And there wasn't any camera.

He sat up to find Sarah moving heavily about the room, sighing over her helpless efforts to tidy its confusion.

Thursty waited until she had disappeared. Then he made a dash for the bathroom. When he came out there was no sign of Sarah or of breakfast. He poked his head into the kitchen. It was empty. Without hope of anything more interesting than a plain boiled egg this morning, Thursty lifted a pot lid. It went clattering to the floor as he stuck a burned finger in his mouth. He stooped to recover the lid, and as he scrabbled under the sink he noticed a rag spotted red. Gingerly, as he would ordinarily never do, Thursty picked it up. Could that be dried blood? He looked at it with a mixture of horror and delight. Perhaps it would be a clue to the thieves. He heard Sarah coming. Hastily he stuffed the stained rag into his pocket.

"Come now, eat yo breakfuss," Sarah said.

Obediently Thursty sat down at the tiny kitchen table. Before him was a boiled egg of the plainest variety, with the white soft to sliminess. The toast was burned. Sarah kept fussing for fear he would disturb Granny. That was the way things were, thought Thursty drearily, wonderful one day and horrible the next. If only he had his kodak!

Since it was Sunday, he could wander over to Pete's or Richy's after breakfast and tell them the whole story, and maybe consult with them about the blood-stained rag. Or should he? Perhaps he could dope it out better alone. Pete was inclined to be smart-alecky and Rich was kind of slow. And besides, thought Thursty, he'd hate to be away when the police came to investigate.

You weren't supposed to move anything. Or touch anything, in case of fingerprints. But last night he and Granny and Sarah, too, had poked around as though it didn't matter a bit. And this morning he had taken that rag. Well, the police never caught on until some keen detective worked it out for them. At least in all the mystery stories Thursty had ever read.

He finished his milk slowly, thinking of these things, wondering how he could manage to stick around till the police came, and not be bored by the enforced quiet. But he had no sooner put down his glass than Sarah shooed him out of the house.

He walked over to Pete's but Pete was still asleep. By the time he reached Richard's apartment, Rich had gone out with his father for the day. Thursty had no ambition to travel further. Gloomily he made his way back to discover that not only the police, but Pop, too, had come and gone in his absence. Worse than that, it had been decided that, starting tomorrow night, until Granny recovered from the shock, Thursty would have to stay elsewhere. He didn't like it. Not that he particularly wanted to stop at Granny's, now that the police visit was over, but where would they park him?

It was actually, after that miserable Sunday, a comfort

to be on the way to school again Monday morning, with
the mysterious rag in his pocket (he hadn't shown it to a soul,
though he had been tempted to scare Sarah with it). That
the question of where he would go when the school day was
over remained unsettled added the small spice of a surprise
in store.

"Hi-ya, Thursty!"

Thursty waved lustily. Of course, everybody remembered
the swell party that Granny had thrown for his birthday, but,
suffering cats, when they heard his true detective story . . . !

Pete and Rich had it first, before class, in exciting fragments. By lunch time all the fellows knew some version of it,
usually with embellishments, as that Thursty had hit at the
robber with his grandmother's cane, but the man, though
lamed by the blow, escaped. Thursty was glad he hadn't
mentioned the stained rag. It could easily have taken on the
proportions of a bloody shroud. Besides, this wasn't something to be jabbered about by the whole Second Form. Not
until he'd figured out some way to handle it himself.

Back in the classroom after lunch, Thursty had the pleasure
of reciting the details all over again.

"It was dark, see, when we got home, and Granny was
sitting there in the foyer while I turned on the light in the
living room. You remember how it looked when we left
for the show, all the pictures and little doodads on the tables,
and the way Granny fussed, how she made Sarah straighten
the scarf on the piano? Well, there wasn't any scarf on the
piano, and all the pictures were gone, at least the ones that
stood around in silver frames, and all those itty-bitty things
Granny's so crazy about, that she's had since forever, and her

bedroom — Golly, it looked as if a cyclone struck it. . . ."

Thursty felt terribly important. Richy's mouth was open as though he could hear better that way, and Pete kept twisting a tuft of his black hair between his fingers the way he did when he was puzzled or excited. The others stood around or sat on the desks with hunched shoulders waiting for what would come next. Only Ernst had a faraway look in his eyes.

And then he suddenly smiled at Thursty, saying in that precise foreign way he had:

"Sure-ly, Thursty, I know how it was. Like when you have a beautiful slide of diatoms and it gets smashed."

"Yeah," said Thursty, without enthusiasm. He hadn't any idea what a diatom was or why you should care if a slide of it got smashed.

"And now Granny's sick," Thursty went on briskly, "and I can't sleep there till she gets over the shock. And I can't go home because of Silly. Maybe I'll have to stay in a hotel!" The words sprang from his lips like Pallas Athene from the head of Zeus as the idea gloriously shaped itself. The very improbability of such an event fascinated him.

"Aw, nerts!" said Pete scornfully. "Think they'd let you stay alone in a hotel overnight?"

"You could stay at my house," offered Richy hospitably, "only since I got my new desk my room's so crowded you couldn't squeeze a cot into it."

"Not standing end up even?" put in Pete slyly.

"You want Thursty to sleep standing up?" asked Richard.

"Sure," Pete laughed. Then his forehead wrinkled. "Gee, fella," he said to Thursty, "you could come over and sleep with me, only there's George!" George was Pete's big brother, a youth so seldom seen as to have become almost a legend, yet possessing on occasion more of a nuisance value than little Silly.

"Why would George mind?" Richard wondered.

"Would you mind if some fella took your bed?"

Thursty was about to enlarge on the possibility of the hotel when Ernst broke in, in a strange voice, as though what he were proposing surprised himself:

"You could come home with me."

"With you!" You haven't got a home, Thursty wanted to say. "But — " he mumbled, hot-cheeked, not knowing how to explain to Ernst the oddity of being invited to stay with a boy who had been invited to stay with other people who hadn't, after all, taken him in. That is, if Granny's story were true. And where was Ernst living, anyway?

"Susi," Ernst half answered Thursty's unspoken question, "can always find room somewhere."

"The girl friend," murmured Pete.

"Thanks a lot," said Thursty, "but I don't know. . . ."

"Wait!" Ernst fished in his pocket and pulled out a small shabby purse. It held a dime. "Can you change it?" he asked. "Then I could telephone. . . ."

"I got a nickel," said Thursty. "Here. You're telephoning for me, fella. It's all right."

Ernst accepted Thursty's nickel and hurried off. The others looked at one another, puzzled and astonished. Ernst had never been so up and coming before.

"Well, now you'll find out about her," declared Pete, after a short silence, "if you do go, that is."

"Who?"

"The girl friend."

"And the place he stays at, there's something screwy about it," said Richy. He stopped abruptly as Ernst pushed open the classroom door.

"She says it's all right if your muzzer is willing," he announced.

"And if your 'muzzer' isn't willing?" asked Pete, in a whisper just loud enough to be overheard.

"Why wouldn't she be?" demanded Thursty, suddenly annoyed with Peter and faintly relieved that the question of stopping alone at a hotel had been eliminated for the time being.

He slid off the desk lid on which he had been sitting, with the intention of going to telephone on his own account, when the bell rang for the close of recess.

The next class was math, for which he was not prepared. How could he have been, what with birthdays and burglars and all? But Miss Mudge, the math teacher, was interested only in the volume of an icosahedron which she was exhibiting with an admiration worthy of a nobler object. And then came a lesson with Andrews in which Thursty was called on to trace the various mountain ranges in the United States on a large blank map. He had the Rockies all right, and the White Mountains, and the Adirondacks, but then Andrews asked:

"And what about the Alleghenies?"

Thursty, not quite sure, decided to take a chance, and placed them precisely where the Berkshires should have been, at which Pete chuckled heartlessly and Richy sympathetically sighed.

"Well, Richard, suppose you show us where that range is," said Andrews.

Thursty handed the crayon to Richy and went back to his seat. Richard sighed again, frowned anxiously, and drew a zigzag line that placed the Alleghenies in the heart of the Ozark country.

It took a whole gym period, with a swift, strenuous soccer game, to erase the memory of those two grim half hours. As Thursty emerged from the shower and began struggling into his clothes, Ernst came over to ask,

"It is oh kay, yes?"

"I got to phone my mother," mumbled Thursty. By this time he didn't quite know whether he wanted to go with Ernst or not. But he would like to find out what sort this Susi person was and what kind of place Ernst might take him to. And if Moth' said "no" to Ernst's proposition, what would she offer instead?

When he telephoned her, with Ernst right beside him, watching him as if he could hear Moth's answers by just widening his eyes, she said, "yes." In fact, she seemed to have arranged it all beforehand with Susi.

Thursty couldn't ask any questions. He just had to accept it. Ernst was standing right there. It was almost, Thursty thought, like being a refugee himself. He had an awkward grin for that notion.

"Why do you smile?" asked Ernst.

"Oh, nothing," said Thursty. "Come on," he said, taking Ernst's arm, "Let's go!"

CHAPTER SIX

Emerging from the draughty subway with Ernst and walking down the cold twilit streets toward strangeness was gloomy and thrilling. It wasn't like having to face Granny's stuffy anxieties, but maybe you'd have to be just as quiet and polite at the place to which Ernst was taking him.

Thursty kept wondering about Susi. Would she be the kind with bright red lips and red nails and a crisp voice that seemed to put you somewhere outside, like Pete's mother, or would she be like Richy's: soft and vague, wispily trailing her speech and her scarves, reminding you of the White Queen in *Alice in Wonderland*? Either way he wouldn't like her.

"There it is," said Ernst.

It was a private house, squeezed in among tall apartment buildings. The door was painted a dark bright blue, and there was the same blue trim on the windows. As they came closer he noticed a swinging sign like something out of an old-fashioned fairy story, big blue and red Gothic letters on a white ground: "THE WELCOME."

Ernst did not ring the bell or lift the brass knocker. He just turned the knob and walked in. Thursty followed.

"It is late," said Ernst. "They have all gone."

Thursty looked at him blankly. Then he took in the little foyer. There were gay colored posters on the walls and photographs of what looked like a children's camp. A few low white chairs for little children stood about, and on a desk, which was overflowing with papers, sat a foreign-looking doll, flanked by a jar of tongue-depressers, and a bottle of iodine. Luggage patched all over with illegible labels nestled in an otherwise empty fireplace. Thursty was trying to decide whether the foyer was most like a kindergarten or a doctor's office or a station waiting room when there was a sound of running and someone at the head of the narrow stairs called down:

"That you, Ernst? Is your friend with you?"

"Yes."

"Fine!"

Thursty scarcely had time to think that it was strange to be called Ernst's friend when there appeared a warm-cheeked, dark-haired young woman, with a smile jolly as an autumn bonfire and an appraising look, as keen as it was brief, in her golden-green eyes.

"So this is Thursty! I am Susi. Welcome to The Welcome."

"Thanks," Thursty mumbled, liking Susi, but puzzled by the small chairs, the luggage and the tongue-depressers, and wondering what next.

"As soon as you are washed, Tante Tilda will give you supper. You must be hungry."

It occurred to Thursty that everyone seemed to think he must be hungry, and that they were generally right. Hastily he stumbled up the twisting staircase after Ernst, glancing curiously into the doorways of the rooms they passed. One had rows of empty cots with folded camp blankets. Another was lined with bookcases and had several small tables with games spread out on them.

In the bathroom washcloths and towels hung on low hooks all around the walls, and over each hook was a tiny picture of some animal.

"That's for the ones that can't read," explained Ernst. "Instead of printed names, each one knows his things by the picture."

What ones? Thursty wanted to ask, dropping into Ernst's manner of speech in his thought. There seemed to be no one about but themselves and Susi and Tante Tilda, whoever she might be. He couldn't figure the place out.

The dining room was in the basement. A large room, it was filled with long tables with benches on either side of them. Supper was set for the boys at the end of one of them. There were bowls of hot soup. And then Tante Tilda, a witchlike old woman with rough gray hair, brought in a platter of sausage and eggs, some dark coarse bread and butter, and a pitcher of milk. For dessert there was only an apple. Susi helped Tante Tilda to carry in the dishes. They were even thicker than those at school. Tante Tilda kept mumbling to herself as she hobbled back and forth, but nobody seemed to mind.

The strangest thing about the place was that Ernst behaved as if he were proud of it all, as if he'd invented it, thought Thursty. And what the heck was it, anyway? A school? But then why cots and washcloths and games? A lodginghouse? But where were the lodgers? And what was wonderful about schools or lodginghouses? Or about the ample but very plain supper? Or about gray-faced muttering Tante Tilda? Or about Susi?

"Your grandmother sent your suitcase over, Thursty, and

I have put it in the room next to mine where you and Ernst are sleeping. Perhaps you want to unpack? It is still too early for The Lone Ranger."

"Thanks."

Thursty scraped his chair back and got up. How come Susi knew about the Lone Ranger? That wasn't like a girl, thought Thursty. But Susi wasn't like a grownup, either. And yet you felt you could count on her. Thursty had never thought so curiously about anyone before.

The room that he was to share with Ernst was small and rather bare. There were just the two cots, a table and a chair, and a dresser with a mangy Teddy bear sitting on top of it. That made Thursty think of Silly. It was all her fault that he had to live in such a hole-and-corner way. And lose his new kodak besides.

There was a snapshot on the dresser: a little white wooden house, with flowering shrubs in front of it, a bicycle leaning against the fence, and a man and woman with arms linked standing on the front step. It was an ordinary snapshot. Thursty couldn't understand why Ernst looked at it and then at him as though he hoped Thursty would say something about it.

"You take that?" Thursty asked, embarrassed by Ernst's look.

"No. Susi did, long ago. But that is our house. That is Mutti and Pappi, my muzzer, I mean, and fazz — father." said Ernst. "Can you bicycle?" he added quickly. "I just started to learn. . . . Do you like to?"

"It's all right," said Thursty, wishing he hadn't noticed

the snapshot at all, and yet certain that Ernst had wanted him to.

He was trying to think of something to say when he heard the familiar opening measures of the Wilhelm Tell overture from Susi's room, just beyond the little passageway. Slapping his thighs to imitate a gallop, he cried out softly: "Hi-yo, Silver!"

It wasn't only the program that made Thursty feel better. Susi's room, where the radio stood, was untidy in a homey, comfortable sort of way, exactly the opposite of Granny's apartment, and yet full, too, of old-fashioned-looking things, like the little cuckoo clock on the wall and the model of the Eiffel Tower that served as a paperweight. There were various foreign-looking dolls on the mantelpiece, and a couple of bulging, shabby letter files. A violin case stood in one corner and a pair of skis in another. When the boys came in, Susi was sitting at the littered table checking a list. She got up, handed Ernst an open tin of cookies, smiled briefly at Thursty, and sat down at her table again with her back toward them.

Thursty dug into the proffered cookie tin and dropped onto the floor next to the radio. Ernst had turned it down so as not to disturb Susi at her work. It was very satisfactory squatting there like that, crunching, with the Lone Ranger's voice coming over the air, the skis in the corner with the promising reminders of winter ahead, and the comfortable presence of Susi, though she excluded them in her absorption. It made even Ernst seem a right guy. Thursty settled down. Only at the back of his mind was the dimming memory of what had happened at Granny's, and, more sharply, the longing to retrieve his kodak. He put his hand in his pocket and just touched the stained rag. It made him feel important and hopeful.

But then almost before he knew it, the villains were caught, the Lone Ranger galloped off, without having done anything to help Thursty with his personal mystery story, and the announcer's voice began its tiresome bright patter.

Susi shoved back her chair, ran her small, plump hands through her dark hair, and smiled the boys off to bed.

Thursty wasn't a bit sleepy, but there was something about Susi — not just the respect for her wishes demanded of a guest and a stranger — that made you do what she suggested. He undressed promptly, and climbed into the cot across from Ernst's. He could tell that Ernst was wakeful too, but somehow he couldn't talk to him, the way he would have talked to Pete or Richy if he had been staying with them. He wanted to find out if Ernst knew how to ski — that would somehow make him feel better about accepting Ernst's hospitality. He wanted to start discussing the burglary again, and hint at the clue in his pocket. Ernst would have liked talking, too. Thursty knew that. But though Susi had thoughtfully closed the door that led to her room, so that they were quite private, neither of them spoke.

Thursty lay staring into the darkness, when he heard the jangle of the doorbell from below. Ernst sat up on one elbow.

"What's the matter, bo?" Thursty whispered. "Expectin' somebody?"

"No," said Ernst, "no, I'm not, it's just — Tante Tilda's so slow," he said, at last. But that wasn't what he meant.

"She's funny, isn't she?" said Thursty, rather because he

was glad to begin conversation on any topic than because of an interest in the old woman.

"You mustn't mind her," said Ernst. "She took care of Susi when Susi was a little girl, and she can't get used to Susi being grown up."

"That's how Delia is with me at home," confided Thursty, "treats me just as if I was Silly's age."

There was the bang of a door, and they could hear Susi's quick feet on the stairs. Ever so faintly sounds came floating up from below: Susi's warm speech and a drawling male voice that sounded oddly familiar to Thursty but was unplaceable. Then for a while there was nothing.

"Say," murmured Thursty, "how would it be if I nipped into Susi's room and saw what time it is?"

"Why not?" agreed Ernst. Whatever he'd been hoping for, it hadn't come.

Thursty slipped out of bed, stumbled through the dark passageway, and blinked about Susi's lighted room.

"Cuckoo! Cuckoo! Cuckoo!" The tiny door flew open, the bird gave three wooden nods, and retired.

Thursty was startled, doubly when he heard Susi and her visitor coming up the stairs. He didn't want to get caught, however innocent a matter it was to be looking at the time and discovering that he and Ernst were awake at a quarter to ten o'clock. He pattered back hastily, forgetting to close the door to the passageway behind him, and jumped into bed just as Susi led the stranger into her room.

"It is perhaps a little cosier here," she was saying. "We shall have coffee as soon as Tante Tilda gets round to it. Now where were we?"

"You were saying you'd let me come in Saturday mornings and show the youngsters how to hold a saw without cutting off their thumbs."

"Hi, Ernie, know who that is?" whispered Thursty, leaning out of bed in a vain effort to see. "That's Andrews! What's he doing here?"

Ernst sat up again, too, shaking his head.

"They'll want to build boats and airplanes," Susi was saying, "and there'll only be enough material for a birdhouse: we're very poor."

"That doesn't bother me. We'll do something," said Andrews. "But I can't come down while school keeps. It'll have to be Saturday mornings or nothing."

"*Na,*" said Susi, and Thursty could feel the smile in her tone, "it won't be nothing!"

"Were you a teacher in Vienna?" asked Andrews.

Susi laughed.

"I! I was a student. I thought some day I would be another Mme. Curie. Instead I became a cook, a nurse, a plumber even, everything you can imagine and some things you cannot imagine."

It sounded like a good story. Thursty was glad he hadn't closed the door. He hoped Susi wouldn't notice.

"But that place — what-d'you-call-it — the —" Andrews fumbled for the name.

"The *Kinderhaus,*" said Susi softly. The word acted on Ernst like a shot. He dropped back onto the pillow and lay very still. But Thursty saw that he was listening hard.

"Ernst's mother," said Susi, "was in charge of it. Ernst went there often. So did his sister, Erica. But it was not meant for them. It was just that they were happy there. It was really a place for workingmen's children to come to after school. They played games. They had their little orchestra. They could get help with their lessons if they needed. I used to help them with their biology. At Christmas there were fine times. In summer there were picnics. *Na,*" sighed Susi, "it was all right."

Thursty had a slight feeling of awkwardness at hearing Ernst's story in Ernst's presence. But his curiosity easily overcame that.

"And Ernst's father," Susi was saying, "was taken to a concentration camp. And his mother fell ill. There was no one to run the *Kinderhaus,* and we could not let it go, not at that time. So I took over. I had never done anything like that before. I was very stupid at it."

Ernst turned slightly in the bed, but said nothing.

"And the house was full," Susi went on. "Every day, every hour, it seemed, there would be a bang on the door, and a child would stand there, crying, not able to talk, to tell us what had happened. Babies. Great boys and girls. From all kinds of homes: factory workers', lawyers', doctors'. Many whose parents were socialists, some liberals, many Jews of course, Catholics. The father had been taken away. The mother was too busy to look out for them. They flocked to us, and we took them all in."

"But where did your funds come from?"

"We ran it — how do you say? — on a shoestring. A broken shoestring. At first there were funds. Wealthy people, who knew their money would be taken away from them by the Nazis, gave it to us instead. But that did not last.

Food was the worst problem. For weeks we lived on spaghetti: spaghetti for breakfast, spaghetti for dinner, spaghetti for supper. And we spread mattresses on the floor for them to sleep. It was like a barrack."

Thursty thought it must have been fun, at that. All those kids. Like a siege. He wouldn't have liked so much spaghetti, not even with meat balls, which Susi hadn't mentioned. But the mattresses. . . .

"I did not see how," Susi was saying, "we could go on. And always I was afraid that the Government agents would make trouble for us."

"Did they?" whispered Thursty, wanting to make Ernst move, or say something.

"Yes," Ernst muttered.

Thursty was glad, partly that Ernst had moved at last, and partly because there was to be more of a story. He was a little ashamed of being glad, because it must have been nasty for Susi, nastier even than the burglary had been for him. But he was eager to hear the rest. He suddenly wished he could forget Ernst. Then it would be just a story, without the interference of what Ernst might be thinking or feeling about it. Thursty hugged his knees tighter, listening.

"Whenever I went out," Susi was saying, "I would be nervous till I got back and found everything in order."

"But it was all right?" That was Andrews.

"*Na,*" said Susi cheerfully, "one day it was all wrong."

CHAPTER SEVEN

"I had been out since morning," said Susi, "running here and there. Usually I telephoned home to ask how things were going, but that day I was too busy. When I got back I saw a notice pasted on the door, like a scarlet fever sign. But it was not scarlet fever. It was a Government order, that the *Kinderhaus* should be closed and everything taken away. I could not wait to read it through, to take out my key and get inside and see. What I saw! Everything was gone — to the last stick of furniture. The children stood about, they sat on the bare floor, staring, doing nothing, not talking even."

"What did you do?" Andrews wanted to know.

"I went out and read the notice again. I saw the official signature, the address of the Chief who gave the order. It was one of the best addresses in Vienna: a palace that had been converted into Government offices. I did not wait. I went there before I could be afraid to go."

"But how —?"

"I tell you I do not know how," said Susi almost impatiently. "Somehow I got past the sentries and the secretaries. I forced my way into the room where the Chief was. You have seen palaces?"

"Can't say I have."

'The Chief's private office was in a room like a hotel ballroom, but of course more magnificent. He sat at the far end. The room was so immense that the big desk seemed very far away. There were tapestries on the wall behind him:

splendid Gobelins. I was shaking so that I did not know how I could walk across the floor to where he sat: it was polished till it shone like his bald head with the light on it."

"You were so frightened?" asked Andrews. It was what Thursty thought, but it was disappointing of Susi.

"I was not frightened. I was shaking with rage. I got across the floor. I stood in front of his desk: it was large, of red mahogany, with a glass top and a great bronze inkwell. He was big too — to fit the room and the desk — in a tight uniform with many medals."

Susi paused. Thursty glanced across at Ernst in the dimness. He was sitting up now, very still. He did not seem to know that Thursty was there.

"What then?" asked Andrews, knocking the ashes out of his pipe.

"*Na,*" said Susi with a short laugh. "I told you I was angry. I did not know how angry until I began to talk.

" 'You!' I said, but I did not say — I shouted. 'Do you know what you have done with your order? You have taken the beds away from under little children! Where will they sleep tonight without a blanket to cover them? Where will they eat tomorrow? Off the floor? Have you no shame!'

"He stared at me. He was astonished that anyone should dare — that a woman, especially, should dare —. I would have been astonished at myself, if I had not been so angry. His eyes were like cold stones. He did not answer me. He turned his head around, stiffly, to the young soldier at attention beside him. I thought he was going to tell him to take me to a concentration camp. I began to be afraid then. He barked something at him. All I understood was that the order was to be remanded. Everything was to be given back to us. The mattresses, the tables, the chairs. The children were to have their things again. The *Kinderhaus* was safe."

Thursty drew a deep breath. That was a swell story. Susi was a swell girl.

"That's great!" murmured Andrews. "But what's the rest of it? How does it patch together? How did you come here and start this?" Thursty could imagine him gesturing round Susi's pleasant untidy room with his pipe in his fist.

"It was the children," explained Susi. "We couldn't keep them. There was no money. There were no facilities. We pulled wires — at last we managed to get permits to send them to England: it was safe there then. At first a few of them" (Ernst and Erica, thought Thursty), "after, many more. I think, altogether, I took five hundred."

Andrews whistled.

"How did you get 'em there?"

"By train, and boat across the Channel. When that got too dangerous, by plane. You see when I crossed the Austrian border the guards would warn me not to come back. But I had to go back, to fetch the others. So next time I crossed at another point. But soon there were no new places to cross, and I was afraid of being recognized. Taking the plane, I went directly from Vienna to Paris, so there could be no trouble at the frontier. And before leaving Paris, I would telephone home, so that if the plane arrived without me, they would know I had been arrested."

"But you weren't?"

"No. But it was a miracle. You see, I had so many commissions. It wasn't just the children. I had to make good

"When I crossed the Austrian border the
guards would warn me not to come back."

use of my time in Paris. I would arrange to meet someone in
a café, on a street corner, who could give me messages to take
back. For instance, they would tell me the hour when there
would be an anti-Nazi broadcast and the radio wavelengths,
so that I could tell them at home. I dared not write anything
down. I had to carry it in my head. And I was always afraid
I would get the numbers mixed up. And then I would have to
see the Quakers, they were so good, the Quakers, to give
them the names of those who most needed to be rescued.
There was so much to do, and no time, and it was necessary
to be very careful, because if I were caught, I could not go on

with my work, and all those children who depended on me, they would not know what to do."

"You've got courage!" said Andrews admiringly.

"No," said Susi in a surprised voice, "I am a terrible coward. When I have to go to the dentist, I nearly die."

"But good Heavens! That was worse than the dentist."

"Oh, no! You see I was too angry to be frightened. It was like that visit to the official who had taken away the children's things. If you are angry enough, you cannot be afraid."

"I don't see," said Andrews, after a pause, "how you do it."

"We are always short, of course," said Susi. "The parents who send us their children can afford to pay very little. They are refugees, living who knows how. The husband cannot find a job. And what can a woman earn sewing or working as a housekeeper? But we manage." Susi paused a moment. "We could get money," she went on, "from rich people here, if we ran things their way. But we would rather do as we please and be poor."

"Where's the rub?" asked Andrews.

"It's this way," Susi explained. "These children who come to us, the little Austrians and Poles and French and Dutch: they have been pulled up by the roots. If you ever tried to transplant anything, you know that you must leave some of the soil it grew in clinging to the roots. *Na,*" Susi laughed, "our rich friends want us to clean off all that old soil with a scrubbing-brush and plant our children's roots straight in American earth. You cannot do that! You know, Mr. Andrews, you cannot!"

Thursty was beginning to piece it together: the foreign children with no place to go, and the washcloth hooks in the bathroom and the cots and the tables with games on them. And Susi, with her anger that did not let her get frightened of things. And Ernst.

And then there were steps on the stairs, heavy ones this time, but not those of a man.

"Ah!" Susi jumped up. "The good Tante Tilda: she brings us coffee."

"Here, let me."

Andrews must be helping Susi clear the littered table. Tante Tilda set down her tray and lumbered out. The friendly aroma of coffee began to mix with the smell of Andrews' pipe and the smoke of Susi's cigarettes. Thursty could almost taste the cakes, or was it sandwiches, that made Andrews mumble between mouthfuls: "This is great!"

Thursty turned to Ernst, whispering:

"Hey, doesn't it make your mouth water?"

"Do you want some?" asked Ernst. "I sink, think, that perhaps Susi . . ."

And suddenly there was Susi, sounding less like a gracious hostess than an outraged mother, exclaiming:

"You are not asleep *yet?*"

But she had a plate in her hand, with cookies on it, and before she went out, closing the door after her firmly, each of the boys had one in his fist.

Thursty could still hear Susi and Andrews talking in the next room, but could not distinguish what was being said. Ernst, too, was silent. Thursty, munching, wondered if Ernst had been in the *Kinderhaus* when the Gestapo took everything away. Golly, it *had* been worse than the burglary. Although, thought Thursty, he'd rather sleep on the bare floor wrapped in a blanket and have his kodak back. Only, thought Thursty, they hadn't had any blankets either. He picked the last crumb off his own blanket and snuggled down in bed. Ernst had swallowed his cookie and lain down without saying a word. He needn't be so stuck up, thought Thursty, even if all those things did happen to him. I bet he never had a blood-stained rag in his pocket!

"Hi, Ernst!" he whispered. He could hold back no longer. "Yes?"

Slowly, in muffled whispers, he told Ernst about his clue. At first Ernst was slow and didn't catch on, but as Thursty explained more carefully he got really excited. Thursty was afraid that at any moment Susi would hear them and come in again. But Andrews went away, and she had to go downstairs to see him out, and after the door banged she was mercifully slow in coming up.

"But," Ernst whispered, when he understood, "but maybe it is not what you think on the rag: maybe it is not blood."

"Rats!" muttered Thursty angrily. "How *can* it not be?" Though he was not so sure. It was just like Ernst to throw cold water that way. It wouldn't be nearly so remarkable if the stain wasn't blood, and it might not be any good as a clue.

"Maybe," Ernst insisted, "it is something else — maybe paint. But listen, Sur — Thursty," he corrected himself quickly. "I can make a test. We scrape off some of the stuff, and I make a slide and put it under the microscope. At school zey will let me use it in free period —" — Ernst was so fascinated by this idea that he did not bother to speak properly. "And I can tell if it is blood or paint, or red ink even."

"Golly," whispered Thursty, "Sherlock Ernst the Great Detective! Maybe you're right, fella, at that."

"If we find the cor — the corp —"

"Corpse?" murmured Thursty dreamily, thinking how rich it would be to unearth a real murder mystery.

"Not corpse, but — corpuscles!" said Ernst. "Zat is ze word — zen we know it is blood. If not, maybe . . ."

"What?"

"Maybe it is still blood. See, if ze corpuscles have dis — dis — ach, I do not know how to say it, but if zey are not zere, still you can tell. It is even more interesting. You put a drop of a solution of zis stuff on a slide, and wiz it some salt, and you boil zem in a drop of acid. . . ."

Thursty wrinkled his forehead. It sounded complicated but jolly, like something really out of Sherlock Holmes. Would they get a chance to do it at school, though, and wouldn't someone come barging in to spoil it all? But still —

"Where'd you learn all about this, fella?" he demanded in a whisper.

"From my fazzer."

Thursty grinned at Ernst's accent, but he felt queer too, thinking of the man in front of the little white house in the sunshine on the snapshot, and the woman with her arm linked in his, and the bicycle leaning against the fence.

It was somehow comforting to hear, then, the small noises that Susi made on her way to bed in the room beyond the passage. Ernst wasn't such a bad guy, thought Thursty, even if he couldn't talk straight, and maybe, thought Thursty, he isn't really stuck up about all that happened to him. He'd seemed excited enough over the stain on the rag. Perhaps they would find the thief and get the kodak back, after all. And then, Thursty said to himself magnanimously, he'd see if Susi had the film of that little snapshot and he'd surprise Ernst with an enlargement. . . . It was too bad the sun was shining right in the father's eyes so you couldn't tell just what he looked like.

Thursty's eyes were all screwed up, as if he were in the picture himself.

"What's the matter?" he mumbled. Someone was pinching his toes.

He opened his eyes. The sun was shining directly in on him. It was morning. Susi was standing at the foot of the cot. Susi was the toe-pincher.

"Time to get up," she said.

It was even odder beginning the day here than it had been at Granny's. There Thursty had felt like a young bull in a china shop. Even Sarah, for all her kindnesses, hadn't let him forget that he was intruding on Granny's sacred privacy. Here everything was strangely public, like a railroad station. There was an intermittent ringing of bells and slamming of doors, and ascending voices in tones of greeting and farewell. Thursty forgot to lock the bathroom door, and looked up startled, the water dripping from his nose and chin, as a small boy barged in, stared at Thursty as at an angry Neptune, muttered a string of unintelligible syllables, and popped out again. It was funny.

Suddenly Thursty dashed out, nabbed Ernst, pulled him along into the bathroom and locked the door decisively.

"Hey, Ernst," he whispered. "You got to make that test for me. And I don't want anyone to know about it, see?

I'm going to give you the rag now. You'll be careful, won't you?"

Ernst nodded.

Thursty took the rag out of his pocket and handed it to Ernst, who folded it carefully and tucked it into his own pocket. Thursty watched him. This was serious.

"Swear you won't blab about it?" he said.

"I don't understand."

"Won't blab, keep it dark, won't tell. . ." Thursty explained impatiently.

"I won't tell," Ernst promised. "But I must say something in the lab, so I can get the microscope and the acid."

"Oh, you make up something, only don't tell 'em where you got the rag, or why you want to make the test. This may mean an awful lot," Thursty assured him.

"I know," said Ernst, smiling gravely. "So you will get your kodak back, maybe. I won't say nossing — anything, I mean."

Thursty shot him another warning look, and quietly unlocked the door.

Now it was Ernst's turn to be important. Still, if nobody else knew about it, it would remain Thursty's secret, and Thursty's discovery.

As they moved down the hall he heard Tante Tilda's grumbling like a ground-bass under the shrill voices of the incoming children. He wondered if she was too busy and cross to provide him and Ernst with breakfast.

He was relieved when Ernst piloted him downstairs to the dining room. As they passed the foyer, Thursty noticed again the shabby luggage piled in the bare fireplace.

When they reached the basement, the dining room seemed like the restaurant attached to a railroad station. There were three children, two of them babies even younger than Silly, sitting at the long tables, drinking milk out of tall glasses with red straws stuck in them. One of them eyed him shyly. The other two kept their eyes fixed on their glasses, clutched their glasses firmly as though something terrible might happen if they dared to pay attention to anything but their morning milk.

And then something terrible did happen. There was a shriek from the foyer, a child's scream, so wild and despairing that the sound was like a pain that made you stop breathing. Ernst's spoon clattered to the floor. Tante Tilda, with a plate of steaming oatmeal in her gnarled hand, stood immobile as though she could not put it down till the cry stopped. One of the babies began to whimper over its milk. The cry went on, thin and high and wild with terror.

Ernst stooped to pick up his spoon. Tante Tilda set the dish of oatmeal down in front of Thursty and went over to the whimpering baby. Thursty stuck his own spoon in the oatmeal but didn't lift it to his mouth. The terrified crying went on. Where was Susi? He couldn't imagine what had happened.

CHAPTER EIGHT

When Silly cried, Thursty could tell by the kind of noise she made whether she were really hurt or frightened or just mad. He could always tell. But this was different. It was only when Ernst began eating his cereal that Thursty, faintly ashamed at being upset, attacked his own breakfast. But he didn't feel hungry. He was glad when Ernst said:

"It's late. We better be leaving."

Thursty followed him out of the dining room without hurrying. He was curious, but he wasn't sure what they would meet in the foyer. The high, wild screams went on.

But there was only Susi, kneeling before a tiny boy, with her arm around him, trying to hush the sounds, too piercing to be issuing from such a small body, that filled the house. And there was another woman, with her hat and coat on, sitting on one of the low white chairs, and holding the boy's hand — she looked like his mother — saying over and over, too low to be heard almost:

"Qu'est-ce que tu as, mon petit, qu'est-ce que tu as?"

The tiny boy could not answer. It reminded Thursty of the time at the farm when one of the dogs was mangled by a hit-and-run driver, and the cruel hours before the vet came to put him out of his misery. There had been no way of comforting the animal, no matter how badly you felt. There was no way of quieting this little boy.

"What's the matter with him, d'you s'pose?" he asked Ernst when they were finally on their way to the subway.

There was no way of quieting this little boy

Ernst shrugged.

"I have never heard one like that. They sometimes cry, when they are homesick or they get hurt, but never like that. Not here. . . ." Thursty knew that Ernst, like himself, was perplexed by Susi's helplessness. It must be something pretty awful if Susi did not know how to stop it.

"Say, Ernst," Thursty came back to his own troubles: "Do you think you'll get a chance to make that test today? About the blood, I mean." As if Ernst didn't know.

"I will try," Ernst promised.

Thursty had to be satisfied with that.

But the fates were against him. Ordinarily, he and Ernst had most of their classes together. He generally saw Ernst at lunch. He played with or against him in gym. But just today Thursty was assigned some special work building scenery for the Thanksgiving festival which took him away from the others. At lunch time Richy and Pete got hold of him to find out if anything new had turned up in connection with the burglary. When they found he had nothing to tell (it was hard work to keep mum about the stained rag), Pete hammered him with questions about the sort of place Ernst lived in and the kind of person Susi was. It was plain to Thursty that Pete didn't really want to know. He just wanted to be confirmed in his dislike of Ernst. Thursty didn't like to disappoint an old friend, but then he was almost beginning to like Ernst in a kind of way. He couldn't make Pete see Susi at all.

And then came gym, and Thursty was put on soccer practice, while Ernst was doing track, so they didn't get together till it was time to go home.

There were two things to be grateful for: this afternoon the class was let out early, so that although chance had separated him from Ernst all day, he did not have to wait unbearably long to see him, and then when they did finally get together it was not in the company of Richy and Pete, so that they were quite free to talk.

"Well?" Thursty demanded as the two of them set off briskly down the hill. "Did you get to the lab?"

"Yes," said Ernst contentedly. "I think it was Susi."

"You crazy! Susi got the blood on the rag?"

Ernst laughed out. It struck Thursty that this was the first time he had ever heard Ernst laugh.

"Susi said Mr. Andrews he should let me use ze lab please in free period, and he asked me would I like. So of course I said yes. And today I was lucky: I had two free periods together. The rest it was not so easy. But I got some help from a Fourth Former. . . ."

"You didn't blab . . . tell him anything?" cried Thursty anxiously, stopping short on the path.

"What should I tell him? Only what acid I wanted, and he helped me wiz part of ze work. But he didn't know why I wanted to do zis, he sought — thought — it was just an experiment for fun."

"Well, and then?" Thursty walked on, relieved.

"I did not think I would get through," as Ernst's self-possession returned, his accent grew fainter, "but I worked almost all lunch period too, and," he wound up triumphantly, "I finished."

"Swell!" cried Thursty. "What did you find?"

"It is not blood."

"Gee!" said Thursty, disappointed. "And I thought —"

"My fazzer always said: if you find out what is not so, you have learned somesing too. Zat is science," said Ernst, his accent coming back with his memories.

"I don't want science," asserted Thursty, slowly climbing the stairs that led to the train. "I want detection!"

"Well, but you have," said Ernst.

"But if you don't know what the stuff is —"

"But I do."

"Then why the heck didn't you say so in the first place?"

"You are in such a hurry, Sursty," Ernst reproached him. After all, his tone suggested, you don't make a test like that every day. It is worth some talk.

But Thursty scowled as he dug his purse out of his pocket and fished for his fare.

"You want to know what it is?" asked Ernst, proud and shy, and passed through the turnstile after Thursty.

"What d'you think?" Thursty stalked angrily ahead into the nearest car. "Who gave you the job anyway?" he demanded over his shoulder.

Ernst waited until Thursty had slumped into a seat and he had sat down beside him.

"It is not blood," he whispered, although they were the only passengers in the car. "It is paint."

"Now what the heck!" Thursty was rather pleased, after all, that Ernst had managed to prolong the mystery, but he was puzzled by his findings. He did wish it had been blood.

All the way downtown in the train he argued with Ernst, who was unhappily eager to discourse on the difficulties and the excitements of the test itself, about how it could possibly be only paint, and what sort of clue to a thief a paint rag offered. Still, it was the one clue they had. He supposed he should tell Granny about it. Or perhaps notify the police, without saying anything to Granny?

He was still wrapped up in his doubts and queries when they emerged from the subway.

"I wonder," said Ernst softly, "if they found out . . ."

"How could they?" demanded Thursty. "They haven't any clue but mine, I'll bet they haven't."

"No," Ernst said, "I didn't mean about ze robbery, I meant about ze little boy."

"What little boy?" asked Thursty. And then, as they hove in sight of The Welcome, he remembered. The little boy whom they had left screaming as though he could not stop. "Yeah," he said, "I wonder."

As before, Ernst turned the door handle and entered without knocking. It was like the farm, thought Thursty, where you leave the door open, as Delia says, to the poor and the stranger.

The first thing he noticed was that the luggage wasn't stuck in the fireplace any more. And then he heard explosive noises and voices from upstairs that, for all the clamor they made, were oddly cheerful. And then Susi looked down the well of the staircase and seeing them, cried gaily:

"Oh, it's you, Ernst! Hello, Thursty!" So that Thursty, although he couldn't feel quite at home, thought again that Susi was a pretty swell girl.

He followed Ernst upstairs to their little room and in a moment there was Susi again, saying, for all the world like Sarah:

"You must be hungry, you two."

"Susi," Ernst interrupted, while Thursty wondered if they would get something different to allay their hunger in this so different place, "Susi, what was it?"

"What was what?"

"The one who cried. This morning."

"Oh." Susi ruffled her hair the way she did when she was puzzled or disturbed. "Poor baby! It was the luggage: the bags Tante Tilda dumped in the fireplace in the foyer. You see," she explained, "he had been in an air raid, the little Michel. It was at the railway station when they were trying to leave Brussels. It came without any warning. And in the confusion, he lost his mother. It was hours before he found her again, and all the time the place was being bombed. So that when he saw those bags with the labels on them, Michel remembered. There had been luggage like that piled up in the station. He thought it was going to begin all over again: the bombs falling in the waiting room and on the tracks, and nowhere his mother. . . . But now," she said, more cheerfully, "the bags have been taken away. He knows this is not a railway station. He knows we are friends. He will be all right."

"Boum!" shouted a child in the room down the hall. "Boum! Boum! Boum! Now you are dead."

"Ach," Susi shook her head, smiling wryly. "And those, they play bombing. It is a good game if you have not seen the real thing."

"But won't he be scared?" asked Ernst.

"Michel, you mean? *Na,*" said Susi, "he is not coming

back till tomorrow. Then they can play visas, instead." And unexpectedly she began to laugh.

"You want to know what is the joke, eh, Thursty?" she asked. "Well, you are a big fellow, you know what it means to get a visa. In Nazi Europe, what it means."

Thursty nodded gravely, feeling quite grown up. He had a vague recollection of stories that he had heard at the dinner table when Pop and Moth' forgot him in the excitement of their rage at what was happening in "Nazi Europe."

"*Na*," said Susi, and it seemed as if she were smiling and frowning at the same time. "The small ones, like Michel, or a little older, they have heard the fathers talking and worry-ing, they know too that it is an affair to get visas, that you are nearly strangled with the red tape. But without a visa, they would not be here at all. Well, so they make a game. I heard them once. There was Karl, he was the official, he was so funny because he wanted to look very stern and how can you look stern with dimples? And there was little Marie, she was asking for her visa, but he would not give it to her. Oh, no. He knew he must make it hard. 'No,' he said, 'I cannot give you a visa today.' 'But why?' asked Marie, and then she said, ach, I have heard them say it so often: 'All my papers are in order. Why can I not get my visa?' Karl did not know what to say. He frowned and sputtered and then he hit on an excuse. 'You cannot get a visa, because, because you have a cold!' "

Thursty grinned.

"Go along now," said Susi, patting their shoulders in dismissal. "Go and see what Tante Tilda has for you."

Thursty was glad to go down to the kitchen with Ernst to find out how Tante Tilda would stay their hunger pangs. The noise of the bomb-players had ceased, and as the boys passed the open door, Thursty saw the children, flushed and panting, sitting in a semicircle, before a young woman with what looked like a guitar on her arm.

"I will sing until you get your breath," she was saying, "and you can come in on the chorus."

Her voice followed them down the stairs, lifted in the familiar tune, though Thursty didn't know the French words to it: "*Malbrough s'en va-t-en guerre. . . .*" And while he and Ernst were munching the thick slabs of rye bread with thin slivers of sausage between with which Tante Tilda, grumbling in a friendly fashion, provided them, Thursty could hear the children shrilling merrily: "*Mironton, miron-ton, mironTAI-ne!*"

It was jolly enough, but queer. Because immediately after, they sang what sounded like a German folk song, and when the boys passed the door on the way back to their room, the children were blithely chorusing: "Home On the Range."

"Where ne-ver is *heard,*" echoed Thursty in a low, firm voice, "a discour-ag-ing *word* . . . Say, Ernie," he broke off, "that was a discouraging word, all right, about its being paint on the rag and not blood. I tell you it makes me know it's going to be harder to catch the thief."

He stopped abruptly as Susi poked her head in at the door to say:

"Your Granny just had Sarah phone, Thursty. It looks as if you could go home tomorrow."

"Golly! Home!" cried Thursty joyfully. "You mean Silly's all better?"

"Oh, Thursty, I am so sorry!" And something in Susi's tone made him sure she meant it with all her heart, so that he had to forgive her, even though he knew she was going to disappoint him with her next words. "I didn't mean home, I meant back to your Granny's. But that's more like home than this, isn't it?" said Susi.

"No," Thursty answered, surprising himself, "it isn't. 'Course," he explained with hasty loyalty, "Granny's as good to me as she knows how. But this place is different, I mean, you can make a racket here, and throw things around. . . ."

"Can you?" asked Susi severely, but there was a twinkle in her golden-green eyes.

"Well, you know what I mean," said Thursty lamely.

"Sure-ly we know," said Ernst eagerly. "That is why Susi called it The Welcome. Couldn't Sursty, Thursty, stay perhaps another while?"

"We'll see," said Susi. "He'll be here tonight, anyway."

"No, but," said Thursty, "I do think I'd better go back to Granny's." He looked significantly at Ernst and plunged his hand into the pocket in which he kept the telltale rag.

CHAPTER NINE

"Well, Dwight." Of course, Granny was glad to see him back, but there was a severity in her creaky voice that made Thursty wish that, since he couldn't go home yet, he might have stayed with Susi. It was partly the effect of Granny's apartment, for, in spite of the fact that the thief or thieves had taken most of her precious knick-knacks, there remained the heavy draperies and the old-fashioned pieces of furniture to give the place, especially in the lamplit dusk, its look of something out of a rich but dead past. Whereas at Susi's everything contributed to a comfortable feeling of here-and-now. The colored posters on the walls were of places it would be fun to visit. You didn't have to be careful of the furniture, or of any precious rugs: the floors were bare. And though a lot of things were old, even the games spread out on the little tables were pretty battered, still it was a friendly kind of agedness, not the annoyingly brittle kind. Besides, Granny always made you feel like a small boy, instead of a young fellow of thirteen-going-on-fourteen, with a downy upper lip and muscles that were the envy of the First Formers and some of the Second Formers as well.

Thursty sensed that he would have to make an impression on Granny at once, or go on feeling like the merest kid, hardly better than Silly. All right, he'd do it. He'd tell her about the painty rag. Maybe then she'd sit up and take notice. Maybe she'd take him seriously then.

With eager awkward haste, because he thought perhaps he should have explained earlier, and he was afraid Granny might ask questions he couldn't answer, Thursty tumbled forth the story of his discovery and Ernst's experiment. At first Granny didn't pay much attention, but when she realized that what he was talking about was no mere schoolboy matter but something that had to do with catching the thief, she leaned forward stiffly in her great chair, clutching the arms of it with her knobby old hands, and looking, in her curbed impatience, like an intent old crane waiting to pounce on its prey.

"Well, Dwight!" she breathed, when Thursty had finished. And then, recovering from her surprise, "it's a good thing you didn't wait any longer to tell me all this. The police just phoned that they got hold of a suspect, who was caught right in this neighborhood trying to sell a camera just like yours."

"Golly!" murmured Thursty. So maybe he'd get his kodak back, after all!

"Tell me, Dwight, about this experiment: what exactly was it that your little friend did?"

Thursty was disgusted at hearing Ernst called his little friend. He wasn't quite sure, either, that he could explain to Granny, not understanding the test any too well himself. It was a relief to have the doorbell ring suddenly and sharply, and a thrill to have Granny exclaim at the interruption:

"Hush! That must be the police now."

She sat very erect, waiting, and then Sarah came in, looking important, to announce that there was a gentleman asking to see Granny.

"Show him in," said Granny in a severe voice.

The gentleman proved to be a plain-clothes man. Thursty decided that he was called a plain-clothes man because there was nothing about his plain suit to make you remember it. Indeed, there was nothing to distinguish him from other people. His voice was agreeable but colorless. He was neither old nor young, neither tall nor short, neither fat nor thin, neither pale nor ruddy. And his name was Smith.

But there was one striking thing about him, and on that Thursty fastened an eagle gaze. He carried a kodak. And it looked like the very one Thursty had lost.

"Sit down, Mr. Smith," said Granny. "I hear you have something to tell us."

"Thank you," said Mr. Smith, accepting a chair. "Yes, I believe I have."

"Have you found my robber?" demanded Granny.

"Perhaps, ma'am. If you'll excuse my correcting you," he added politely, "the term is burglar. Robbery involves violence. I believe there was no violence in this case?"

"Well!" exclaimed Granny, "I don't know what else you'd call it when you come home to find your home a wreck and a ruin and all your most valued possessions gone."

"But the burglary was committed in your absence, was it not?" persisted Mr. Smith.

"Do you think I'd have stood quietly by and let them walk off with my things?" Granny sniffed. But then she thought better of it and said, "Oh, I see your point, young man, they didn't hit me over the head first because I wasn't home to be hit. But they did practically everything else. Now about this burglar. Did you catch him? Did you get my amethyst brooch and my ivory curios and — well — and all the other things?"

"So far," said Mr. Smith, "we have only one of the stolen objects."

Thursty's heart began thumping strongly. He kept his eyes fixed on the kodak as though to remove them would be to let it vanish again.

"We seem to have the kodak mentioned in your inventory."

"Dwight's kodak, yes," said Granny. "How did you get that? And nothing else?" she added sharply.

"It is a curious story."

"Yes?"

"Well," said Mr. Smith, "one of the men on the force has had his eye on a store in this neighborhood for some time. It is to all intents and purposes a pawnshop. But the pawnbroker is suspected of being a fence."

"Now what's that?" asked Granny.

"A receiver of stolen goods."

"Well, I never!" cried Granny. "Why don't you lock up the fellow and close the place? Although maybe it's just as well, because then you'd find it harder to locate the robbers — burglars, I mean."

"Aside from that," said Mr. Smith, "we can't get the goods on these people so easily. They're a tricky lot. But the point is this. When a burglar makes a fairly big haul, the sort that he got here, you can be sure he won't dispose of the valuables right away. He'll get rid of something of small importance, first. Like this kodak."

Thursty was indignant, but there was nothing he could say.

"And here," Mr. Smith went on, "was this painter-fellow. . ."

"Eh?" cried Granny.

"Oh, I'm sorry. I forgot to say that the suspect appears to be a painter."

"Dwight!" cried Granny. "Speak up."

Thursty got hot and red, and felt as though his heart were quite literally beating in his throat. But he managed somehow to get his story out, and in the end he produced the paint rag from his pocket, and Mr. Smith took it and looked at it as though it were Exhibit A in a murder mystery.

"That's circumstantial evidence," he said.

Thursty grinned happily.

"Only trouble is, I don't see why he'd be carrying a paint rag around with him when he was committing burglary. He's not a house painter, either," said Mr. Smith.

"Must be like your Uncle Tom," put in Granny.

Just as Thursty was beginning to despair of ever getting his kodak into his hands again, in spite of the fact that he had produced the evidence that clinched the matter, Mr. Smith got up and turned it over to him. Thursty fairly grabbed it out of his hands, and examined it eagerly, noting all over again, as he had on his birthday morning, the shining gadgets that made it the swell kodak it was.

"The fellow's got a pretty good story, though," said Mr. Smith, turning to Granny. "This Armand, as he calls himself. Seems to be a French refugee, or poses as one. Says he's awfully hard up. Got a wife and child, a little girl, name of

Marguerite, I remember: he kept talking about Marguerite. His wife goes out dressmaking, she doesn't make much, and he hasn't been able to find any work. He can't go out looking for a job — says he wants to do commercial art work — because of the kid: he can't leave her alone in the lodging-house. He decided he'd better sell something. Only thing he had was his kodak, a good one he'd brought from the other side. And he took it to this fence. That's how we got hold of it. Well, sir," Mr. Smith finished, "if that's your camera, Armand'll have to make up a better yarn. How about it, son?"

"Dwight!" said Granny impatiently. "Why don't you answer?"

But Thursty couldn't say anything. He turned the kodak over again. It was no use. The range finder that had been the chief marvel of his kodak was missing. This just wasn't his. He was as badly off as before he'd found the paint rag, or before the cop had landed on that French refugee or whatever he was. Wordlessly Thursty handed the camera back to Mr. Smith.

"What is it, son?" he asked. "Not yours, after all?"

Miserably Thursty shook his head.

"Nope," he said.

"What a shame!" cried Granny. "Then I suppose my amethyst brooch is gone for good."

"Oh, I wouldn't say that, ma'am," said Mr. Smith gently. "But it looks as if maybe this Armand's story were true, after all."

There was a short silence, during which Thursty kept swallowing something hard and nonexistent. It was really a rotten shame, to nearly get his kodak back, and then not.

"Poor fellow!" sighed Granny.

Thursty thought she was talking about him. He was feeling particularly sorry for himself when she poked him with her cane and said:

"Wake up, Dwight! What is the name of that place?"

"What place?"

"I hope, Dwight, your memory's not as bad at thirteen as mine is at seventy-three. The place you were stopping at with What's-his-name."

"Ernst? It's called The Welcome," said Thursty.

Mr. Smith, looking a little puzzled, pocketed the paint rag, for no good reason that Thursty could see, although now he was rather glad to forget about his false clue, and started to take his departure.

"I'm sorry to have troubled you for nothing," he said to Granny. "Sorry to disappoint *you,* young man," he turned to Thursty.

"Not for nothing," said Granny. "If that man's story is true, about himself and his wife and his little girl —" She broke off. "Don't you think, Dwight," she said then, "it might be a good idea?"

And suddenly in the midst of his private distress at having lost his kodak a second time, as it were, Thursty recognized that Granny had lit upon a solution of the unemployed painter's problem. And he found himself explaining to the plain-clothes man all about The Welcome and Susi, and what she did for the boys and girls who came to her.

"Well," said Mr. Smith, "I don't care much about making things easy for wrong guys. But this fellow Armand, I guess maybe he's telling a straight story at that. And I'd like to make it up to him for our mistake. It's not a cinch for these refugees. I've run into more than one of them — not in the way of business," he explained carefully. "Happens I live in a neighborhood where a lot of them hang out. They have a tough time of it all right."

Mr. Smith, having made a pencil note of Susi's address, tucked his notebook into his pocket, and the camera that wasn't Thursty's under his arm, and made his exit.

Thursty was left alone with Granny, a faint curiosity as to whether Marguerite would be put into Susi's capable hands, and a great wonder as to where his own kodak really was.

CHAPTER TEN

Thursty woke the next morning with a curious feeling of missing something, without knowing, in the first sleepy minutes, just what it was. Sitting up in bed, awake, aware of the need to keep from disturbing Granny, he wondered vaguely if he could be missing The Welcome, with Ernst companionably tearing into his clothes beside him, and maybe a scramble as to who would get to the bathroom first. But as he forced himself to get out of bed and dashed to close the window, he realized that what he missed was the painty rag and the hopefulness that the touch of it had always brought him. The false alarm last night had been a mean disappointment. And now the precious rag was in the hands of the plain-clothes man. The police didn't seem to be too bright, picking up a poor refugee for trying to sell his own camera, even if it was in a crooked shop. To make matters worse, Thursty suddenly recalled that there was going to be a meeting of the Camera Club after school, and he had nothing to show. Slowly he pulled on his clothes, glumly he contemplated his solitary breakfast. The Welcome had been like home at least in this, that there had been a stir about the place from the moment you awoke, with Ernst there to tease or to talk to, and floating up from below the voices of the early ones, whose mothers, before going to work, brought them to Susi, and even Tante Tilda, for all her apparent grumpiness, not treating you as Sarah did: like an incarnate noise that had to be constantly shushed.

Thursty sat down at the corner of the kitchen table, Sarah having decided that this would be less disturbing to Granny

than if he ate in the living room. It was crowded in the tiny
kitchen, what with Sarah's great bulk and uneasy move-
ments. Thursty had finally to notice them, in spite of his
concentration on his own troubles.

"What's the matter, Sarah?" he asked, mopping up the
last of his egg with a bit of buttered toast.

"Ah don't know what on earth Ah done wid mah rag,
that's what. Seems to me them robbuhs steal 'eve'y thing
they kin fine. What good that rag do them, heh?"

"They couldn't have stolen your dishrag, Sarah," said
Thursty.

"Not mah dishrag, boy. It's mah rag Ah wuz wipin' mah
brush on when Ah paint the twine box red to match mah
kitchin trim." Sarah went on muttering something or other,
but Thursty, his glass of milk half way to his mouth, heard
no more.

"Sarah!" he said, so sharply that Sarah immediately
shushed him. "Sarah," he repeated, more quietly, but with
a kind of melancholy rage, "you missing a *paint* rag?"

"Been missin' it since the robbuhs wuz heah."

"I guess," said Thursty feebly, setting down his milk and
rising from the table, "I guess you'll find it all right, Sarah.
I got to go now. I'm late."

He wasn't late, at all, as a matter of fact. He was so early
that though he got into the first car of the subway train, he
met none of the gang. He slumped into a seat, thinking how
mean it would be to explain to Ernst that all the work he had
done in the lab he had done for nothing, on Sarah's old paint
rag. Luckily, the others knew nothing about it, but Thursty
hated the thought that they might find out. Maybe, Thursty

said to himself, he'd better not even let Ernst in on the story. But Ernst would want to know what had happened. Oh, the heck with it!

The day that had begun so badly held to the same ugly tenor. Thursty managed to avoid Ernst before class, but he kept hearing fragments of talk about the meeting of the Camera Club that reminded him of his loss, and then in the middle of the morning Andrews announced that they were to have an examination in history. Thursty had no one to look to for sympathy. Richy, who might have shared his dismay at the news, had hurt his hand in gym and was excused from all writing. Pete was a whiz at names and dates. The others would come out all right, like Jim Clark, or, like Fatty Rossiter, they were too easygoing to mind if they didn't. Ordinarily, Thursty would have taken the exam in his stride. But what with Silly's measles and Granny's burglar, he hadn't been doing much studying since term began, and to-day he was so down that an unexpected exam seemed a heavier load than he could bear.

The examination paper was full of tricky questions like: Which Adamses held what high positions in the United States Government? Thursty was one of the last to finish. He had a blot on one page, for which he was rather grateful, because then Andrews mightn't be sure that the date it blurred was wrong. It was funny, but the series of firms that had acted as sponsors for The Lone Ranger stuck in his head much more readily than the names in the history book.

Thursty wasn't sorry to have been slow, however, if it meant that Ernst had gone on to the next class, and wasn't hanging around waiting for him. He was afraid that Ernst would get out of him, against his will, the humiliating story of the paint rag.

But there was no getting rid of him. There he was, just outside the door, waiting. Thursty tried to ignore him, but Ernst called out eagerly:

"Thursty! I have such a thing to tell you!"

"What? That the exam doesn't really count?"

"Nothing with the exam. About what you did last night. Susi said me — told me, that it must thank you, because without you they would never have found out. And now it will be so much easier for them, it is just what they needed, it was so lucky. . ." Ernst had babbled on happily, but more and more quietly as he noticed that Thursty was not paying attention to what he was saying. Now he stopped altogether, looking at Thursty wonderingly.

"What are you gabbing about?" Thursty asked.

"The father of Marguerite. The one you sent to Susi."

"Oh." So Ernst did know, then, about the policeman's blunder.

"The Welcome's a good place for the kid to stay during the day," Thursty admitted, "while her mother's working and her dad's looking for a job."

"Sure-ly," said Ernst with quiet conviction. "But Thursty —"

"Come on, fella, we're late for shop," Thursty interrupted hastily. He didn't want to hear any more about the little Marguerite, who must be just a kid like Silly, or about her father, who brought up such unpleasant memories. He didn't want Ernst asking embarrassing questions.

Ernst didn't seem to understand how Thursty felt. And

Thursty, eager to keep off the subject of the paint rag, pretended an interest in the Frenchman and the little Marguerite which he was far from feeling. All right: the Armands lived in two rooms in a lodginghouse around the corner from The Welcome. And Mme. Armand went out dressmaking or something. And M. Armand couldn't go looking for a job because he couldn't leave Marguerite alone. So what? Now Marguerite was going to be left with Susi every day and everything was lovely. But not for Thursty.

At last it was lunchtime and he was able to forget his troubles over beef and potatoes and spinach. But he was vaguely worried about the exam.

"Which Adams was which?" he asked Peter, who was sitting next to him, busily stuffing mashed potatoes into his mouth.

"Plain John, John Quincy, Charles Francis," chanted Pete as soon as he could speak. "It's easy. John Adams, second president of the U. S.; John Quincy, his son, sixth president; Charles Francis, *his* son, minister to Great Britain during the Civil War. There were some more of 'em, but those were the important ones."

"I thought Charles Francis was president of a railroad," said Thursty, wrinkling his forehead.

"That was another one," said clever Pete.

"And what about Henry? I've heard my dad talk about a Henry: he was some kind of educator," put in Richard tentatively.

"Oh, he just wrote books," said Pete.

"Yeah, I've heard Pop talk about Henry, too," said Thursty. "But I don't remember what he said."

"He wrote books," Pete finished, "because *my* father has 'em: I saw 'em on the same shelf with the American history stuff when I was looking something up for class."

"My dad's long on American history, too, 'specially Lincoln," said Richy. " 'Member last Fathers' Day, when they quizzed the fathers, and your dad came out on top?" he asked Thursty.

"You bet! Hope they have it again this year," said Thursty, slightly cheered by the recollection, and looked up to see if dessert were on its way into the dining room. Across the table he caught Ernst's eye. The fellow had the same faraway strange look he had worn during the first days. Guess he must have flunked, thought Thursty.

"The fathers were all right on history and math," said Pete, "but golly, when it came to English. . ."

"But," said Ernst softly, "English is their language, no?"

"No," said Pete. "English isn't a language, it's a subject. It's prepositional clauses and the-quality-of-mercy-is-not-strained, and all about Kelley and Sheets, I mean Shelley and Keats. . . ."

They gave Pete the laugh he was looking for, and Thursty began spooning up his dessert, which was canned cherries.

"How many you got?" asked Pete. "I've got twelve."

Thursty counted, not forgetting the two pits.

"Fourteen."

"How many you got, Richy?"

"M'mm, fourteen."

"I've been gypped!" cried Pete, more in sorrow than in anger.

But it was Thursty who felt cheated. He kept thinking

about the coming meeting of the Camera Club and how he wouldn't be able to show off his kodak.

"What you fellas doing this week end?" he asked, in an effort to find a cheerful subject of conversation.

"I'm going to the ball game," said Pete. "My dad told me this morning he bought tickets."

Yes, thought Thursty, and Pop would have, too, if I'd reminded him, only how could I when I don't see him at all, and it's always Moth' who's on the phone nights, wanting to talk to Granny. Dimly he heard Pete enlarging on the difficulty of getting tickets at the last moment.

"What you doing, Rich?"

"Guess we'll go to the country."

If Silly hadn't had the measles, they might all have gone off to the farm, too, Thursty reflected. He was thinking what a nuisance Silly was, when Ernst piped up:

"I am going to see my sister!"

"What do you know about that!" exclaimed Pete sarcastically. "Going to see your sister! Well, isn't that wonderful!"

It occurred to Thursty that, for Ernst, seeing his sister probably *was* something rather special. She was his twin, not a baby like Silly. Besides, except for Susi, she was the only person out of New York's seven millions with whom Ernst was really at home. Thursty vaguely realized all this, but the milk of human kindness had quite soured in him. He couldn't side with Ernst against Pete. He opened his mouth and shut it again without saying anything. Just then the bell rang. There was a scraping of chair legs being shoved back from the tables, a shuffle of feet, and a rising clamor of voices as the boys left the dining room.

Thursty had no difficulty in avoiding Ernst the rest of the afternoon. Indeed, it was almost as if Ernst were trying to keep out of his way. So much the better.

He had a hard time making up his mind whether or not to go to the meeting of the Camera Club. True, it was the one bright spot in a dismal day. But what fun would it be, when he had nothing new to show? Still, they'd all go down to Cohen's Soda Shoppe afterwards. Thursty wondered if he should order a chocolate frosted or a pecan marshmallow sundae. The frosted would last longer but the sundae would taste better. He decided on the sundae, and made for the club meeting on the run, for he was late.

"'Lo, Thursty." "Hi-ya." "Looky, what we got here."

The boys were hunched over a small photograph.

"What is it?"

"Ask him." Fatty Rossiter, the heaviest boy in the Form, pointed a thick finger in the direction of Ernst.

"What is it?" Thursty repeated, surprised, examining the picture Fatty handed him. It was an arrangement of fancy shapes, something like magnified snow crystals, but dark.

"Diatoms."

"What the heck are diatoms?" demanded Thursty.

"Ocean plants. The fish eat them."

"Whyn't we use 'em to catch fish then?"

"But Thursty," Ernst laughed, "you cannot see them but with the microscope."

"How'd you photograph them then?"

"It was not easy," said Ernst. "I had to work with Susi's camera and that is not for microphotography. And the light was not as strong as I needed. But it came out good, no?"

"Yeah," Thursty admitted. "They're pretty, all right." When'd you do it?"

"It was just before I made the blood test. . . ."

"What blood test? What's Ernie up to, anyhow?" Pete wanted to know.

"Oh, zat was nossing," Ernst stammered, meeting Thursty's scowling look. "But zis photograph, I would like some day to show you. . ."

"What's the good of photographing something you can't see?" asked Thursty, angry at Ernst for having dropped a hint about the test and eager to head off the boys' questions.

"But diatoms are interesting," said Ernst. "And important."

"To fish," said Pete.

"To us." And when Thursty laughed, Ernst added defensively: "But truly, Sur — Thursty. If there are not many diatoms, and some years there are not, then the little fish go hungry. So they die. So the big fish who feed on them starve, too. The fishermen catch only a few. And fish costs more on the market, and the poor people cannot afford, and they do not get." He paused. "I did not think of all this. My father said me, told me it." He paused again, before he said, slowly: "Things you cannot see make sometimes a big difference."

"Mm . . . yes," said Thursty, and was glad that the last bell rang, and the meeting would have to break up. Ernst was getting just a bit too much attention. First thing you knew, the fellows would begin asking him what he'd meant by that reference to the blood test. Then the whole story would come out. And Dwight Thurston, Jr. would look plenty foolish.

Richy and Pete, perched next to Thursty on the high stools in Cohen's Soda Shoppe ten minutes later, were in full agreement on the score of Ernst's sudden cockiness.

"The way that Ernst Keller talks, you'd think it was a Science Club," complained Richy, "instead of a Camera Club."

"The poor fish," said Pete. "That's a pun, fellas, — laugh: Or Else!"

Richy and Pete perched next to Thursty on
the high stools

Thursty grinned weakly.

"He's all right," he said, feeling more humane after his third mouthful of vanilla ice cream, sirupy chocolate and crunchy pecans. "But —"

"But!" Pete caught him up sharply. "Guy that takes pictures of fish food! Guy that can't even talk English!"

"We ought to give him a little hazing maybe," suggested Richard gently.

"Class is going on a bus excursion around the city tomorrow. We might get a chance then," said Pete.

"Maybe," said Richard hopefully.

Thursty, scraping the chocolate off the sides of the dish with his spoon, said nothing.

CHAPTER ELEVEN

Thursty relished excursions. You never knew what might turn up. Like the time that the class ferried over to Staten Island to study the geological formations there, and stopped for lunch at a funny old inn where the pancakes were as big as a tea tray and the waitress had asked if they wanted light beer or dark. And the time, way back when they were little kids, that they were taken to see a firehouse, and Pete slid down a pole when no one was looking and landed in a water bucket.

Today the whole class was to pile into a couple of chartered buses and cruise about Manhattan for the day, "for to admire an' for to see, for to be'old this world so wide," as Pop said when the family went traveling. Thursty noticed with pleasure that Pete had come generously provided with peanuts and chocolate bars to while away the duller stretches of the trip. Richy had his camera along. And Ernst was carrying a Mason jar, an unlikely object which he handled as tenderly as if it were brimming with nitroglycerin. Only it was empty.

"What you got that along for, Ernie?" demanded Pete. "Going to bottle some air from the other end of the island?"

"No, but some water maybe," said Ernst, smiling.

"Whatever for?"

"To see under the microscope what is in it."

"Oh." Pete lost interest.

They jounced along for some time without much talk, except when Andrews reminded them of the landmarks he had told them about. It was queer to think that the college campus they would soon pass had been a bloody buckwheat field in Revolutionary War days, and that they were on their way to the very spot where Washington had taken his oath of office.

The first really strange section for Thursty was the beginning of Harlem. The wide streets were crowded with dingy tenements and shops flaunting enormous crazy signs. The look of the streets and of the dark-faced men and women walking there made Thursty feel as if he were in some foreign city.

Glancing across to the opposite window of the bus, he caught sight of the back of Booker's dark woolly head. Of course, thought Thursty uncomfortably, Booker doesn't live in this slum. Nevertheless, he wondered how soon they would get out of Harlem and into one of the other peculiarly individual regions of New York that Andrews had mentioned. He wouldn't feel quite the same about the Ghetto or Chinatown or Little Italy.

"Hi," Peter nudged him as the bus swung round a corner. "Looky!"

Thursty peered over Peter's shoulder.

"I don't see anything but a girl in a red hat."

"That's what I mean, jerk," retorted Peter, who pretended, in imitation of his brother George, an interest in the fair sex.

"Girls!" said Thursty scornfully.

"If you had a sister. . ." Ernst began.

"What about Silly?" asked Thursty.

"I mean your own age," said Ernst, "like Erica."

"Sisters don't count," said Pete decisively.

"Maybe Silly doesn't," said Ernst, "but Erica —"

"What do you mean: Silly doesn't?" asked Thursty, not because he thought so much of Silly, but because Ernst had no right to assume that he had something better in the way of sisters than did Dwight Thurston, Jr.

"O captain, captain, stop the ship, I want to get off and walk!" sang out Richard.

"What's the matter with you?"

"Nothing. Only if we'd stop somewhere I could take some snapshots," said Richy, patting his camera.

Thursty was disgruntled. Here was Richard with his camera. And he without even the hope of getting his kodak back. And Pete, that shrimp, feeling superior in the reflected glory of his brother George's sophistication. And Ernst, who sat there, clutching his empty Mason jar, babbling about his twin, Erica, whom nobody had ever seen.

"Can't we get some fun out of this trip?" Thursty asked Peter.

"Wait till we get downtown and have a chance to walk around," said Pete.

"No, but," said Thursty, "I mean real fun: getting somebody's goat or something."

"Why, sure," Pete grinned. "Here, Ernie, have some," and he held out the peanut bag.

"Thank you!" said Ernst, as much pleased to be counted one of Pete's intimates as to be offered refreshments.

He plunged his fingers eagerly into the bag, to encounter nothing but broken shells.

"I — I am afraid zere are none left," he said.

"Sure zere are," said Pete, parroting his accent.

"No," said Ernst, with a small smile, to show that he wasn't too badly disappointed: "only shells."

"Well!" cried Pete brightly, "I didn't say, 'Have some peanuts,' did I? I just said: 'Have some.' Have some shells!"

Thursty burst out laughing at Ernst's face. Peter, the clown, didn't even smile.

The rest of the trip was uneventful, except for the mild thrill of seeing the façades of the great transatlantic docks, when they finally reached West Street, with here and there an enormous liner being painted battleship gray, and the mixed smells in the neighborhood of Washington Market. And then finally they were at the Battery, and could pile out and stretch their legs.

Half of them made for a point where they'd see the Statue of Liberty, holding her giant torch over the bay. But Andrews soon herded them together again and was telling them about the old Aquarium in the days when it had been a fort, and an amusement place, and an immigrant station.

Thursty glanced across the park, with its statues and flag-poles, its scattering of water-front vagrants and mothers and small children on the park benches, down toward the tower of the Fireboat Station, and then up to the mass of Whitehall and the terraced office buildings. It was hard to think of the Indians and even the Dutch as ever having any part in this place. He tried to imagine Washington pacing along the sea wall but it just wasn't real, and as for the other people whom Andrews mentioned: Lafayette, and Jenny Lind, and Morse with his telegraph, and Verrazano, who had come here by accident when he was looking for Asia, they were just so many waxworks.

He was recalled to the present by Andrews saying:

"See that flagpole?"

The boys nodded. How could they help seeing it, Thursty wondered, when it stuck up like that?

"When the British had to evacuate New York," said Andrews, "they left the royal flag flying, and they greased the flagpole so no Yankee could climb up and pull it down. But there was a bit of a sailor lad who shinned up the pole, grease and all, and tore down the British flag. The Stars and Stripes have been flying up there ever since."

"Golly, I'd like to try it," murmured Thursty, tired with so much exposition, and longing for a little action.

"Now we'll get a sniff of the Fulton Street Fish Market, if we have time," said Andrews.

Ernst's face fell.

"You want to see South Street," said Andrews, trying to ease off his disappointment. "That's where the sailing ships used to dock in the old days. You'll find barges docking there now, with fussy little tugs warping them in, and ship chandlers' shops and maybe even a tattoo artist."

"I'll bet there's pictures to take on South Street," said Richard eagerly.

"When do we eat?" muttered Thursty. Enviously he eyed Richy, who had skipped off to the waterside to get a good view of the Fire Fighter berthed below the Fireboat Station. Andrews had said the 130-foot boat could throw a stream of water over Washington Bridge.

"What's the fun," Thursty asked Peter glumly, "if you can't see the thing in action?"

"Makes you want to commit arson," Pete agreed.

And then they were in front of No. 7 State Street, and Richy was taking a snapshot of the mission that had been a mansion two centuries ago. It seemed to Thursty that wherever they went Richard was busy with his camera. Now it was a couple of stevedores at work, now a barge rigged out as a houseboat, with the family wash hung up to dry and flowerpots on the window sills. And once it was what looked like a cross between a junk shop and a country store, the bleary window filled with all kinds of ships' tackle and curious knickknacks.

"That was a neat one!" Richard kept saying. Thursty knew he was right, and ached over the fact that he hadn't been the one to snap it. And then Pete, whose father had a seat on the Stock Exchange, asked importantly if they would get to that point of interest. And there was Jim Clark, whose father had a law office in the neighborhood, and who kept talking about a lunch he'd had at Fraunces Tavern. Another boy's father was a journalist who had taken him through the newspaper district and yet another had a parent at City Hall. Booker announced that they weren't far from Bartel's Bird and Animal Company, where you could buy anything from a white mouse to an elephant: he knew because he had an uncle who worked for a circus, and that was where they got some of their animals.

Thursty felt increasingly out of it. Bartel's and City Hall and newspaper row and the Stock Exchange were as foreign to him as if he came from another city, as if, indeed, he were an outsider, like Ernst.

As a matter of fact, Ernst, the foreigner, seemed to know more than Dwight Thurston, Jr., the suburbanite. The year

Ernst had spent knocking around London alone with Erica he had picked up odd bits of information about the British capital that kept coming out every time Andrews told the boys something about New York, like pieces of chocolate out of a slot machine. Ernst was getting altogether too much attention. It was like yesterday at the Camera Club, when he'd brought in that picture of dia — whatever they were. Thursty recalled that afterwards, at the Soda Shoppe, Peter and Richy had agreed that Ernst needed taking down. And that the excursion would probably provide an opportunity for it.

As they turned back to resume their bus ride, Thursty caught up with Pete and, linking his stout arm in Pete's thin one, pulled him off to one side.

"Hey, Pete."

"Yeah."

"Aren't we going to do something?"

It took a minute or two to make Peter understand that Thursty meant to do something about Ernst. The time had come to put him in his place. Peter took it under advisement. There didn't seem to be much they could do.

Unexpectedly, the opportunity offered itself.

They were back at the Battery again, ready for a trip to a part of the city that they could not reach on foot. Ernst, still clasping his Mason jar, came to the realization that they were leaving the water front for the day. He dashed across to the shallows where the water was muddiest and richest in invisible life. Andrews, busy pointing out the direction of Bowling Green, didn't notice.

"It used to be a hog and cattle market. And then it was

a parade ground for the Dutch militia. And later on the British leased the spot to three citizens who wanted to bowl there. Know what the rent was?" Andrews laughed. "One peppercorn a year!"

Still laughing, he bundled the boys into the buses.

"All here?" he asked. "Better count noses."

It was then that Thursty had his inspiration. He'd work it so that Andrews would count him twice, once for himself and once for Ernst. Ernst, down by the waterside, was evidently having trouble filling his precious Mason jar, or perhaps he was exploring a more likely spot than the one he'd started for. If they were off and away before Ernst got back, wouldn't he be flabbergasted!

Thursty, safely ensconced, leaned over and whispered his ruse to Pete.

"It's a cinch," said Pete. "If Andrews doesn't spot him, maybe he'll think he's in the second bus. Golly, I hope we start soon!"

"One," counted Andrews, "two, three, four — I thought I counted you before, Thursty," he said.

Thursty grinned. If Andrews had asked directly: Didn't I count you before? he'd have had to say, yes. But this way — well, it was a white lie, maybe, cream-white. . .

And while he was thinking about it, the driver shifted gears and with a soft roar, the bus was on its way. Ernst was not.

CHAPTER TWELVE

Thursty punched Pete with delight as the bus swung away from the Battery. This was really something. He could just imagine Ernst's face as he turned round with that Mason jar of his to discover that they had left without him.

"Have some shells!" he chortled. "Maybe he'll have some sea shells for souvenirs."

Just then, perhaps because they were in the neighborhood of Bartel's, Booker turned round and asked,

"Where's Ernie?"

"Ssh!" Thursty hushed him up swiftly. "Don't let on, Booker, but Ernie's not here at the moment. He's keeping an appointment with some fish food."

It took a moment for Booker to get the drift of what Thursty was saying.

"How'll he ever find us?" he asked then.

"Oh," said Pete airily, "didn't you hear him tell about how he went all over London alone with Erica? Now he'll discover New York. Live and learn! Join the Navy and see the world!"

"But," Booker objected gently, "that's tough on the kid. Maybe he hasn't even got carfare."

It occurred to Thursty that Ernst never accompanied the crowd to the Soda Shoppe, not permitting himself the extravagance of so much as a coke. Thursty wasn't too clear about the Manhattan subway system. It might take more than one subway fare for Ernst to get back home. When Andrews turned round to tell the busload of boys that they were to have lunch in Chinatown, Thursty did not join in the whistles of pleasure that greeted the announcement. He just didn't feel hungry. He supposed it was the chocolate bar he'd eaten and all the peanuts. Ernst had been gypped out of peanuts too. The bus seemed to be going at an awful clip.

Thursty wondered how soon Andrews would notice that Ernst was missing: when they got out to eat or only after? Andrews wouldn't really need to know who was responsible. He might think it was Ernst's fault for having dashed off to fill the jar, or his own carelessness in counting the boys when they had piled into the bus on leaving the Battery.

"Say, Thursty," Booker leaned over to put his arm about Thursty's shoulder. "Would you mind awfully if I let on that Ernie ain't here?"

Thursty felt a sudden warmth of affection for Booker. Then Andrews would find out, and do something about it, and nobody would get in Dutch.

But just as he was about to urge Booker to go to it, he was overcome with a queer feeling which seemed to be lodged somewhere in his stomach, that made him shake his head. It wasn't that he didn't want Booker to tell. On the contrary. But after all, it wasn't Booker's job.

The bus drew to a stop at a corner that gave on a narrow street, filled with crazy tenements leaning over shops even odder than those they had seen on South Street. And there was the Chinese restaurant, sending its strange inviting odors into the cool autumn air.

Andrews, waiting for the second bus to unload its passengers, glanced casually at his own charges and stated, rather than asked: "All here."

Thursty was conscious of a thick throbbing in his throat and an unpleasant heat in his cheeks. He did not look straight at Andrews as he blurted out: "No."

"No what?" asked Andrews.

"No, sir," said Thursty, getting even redder.

"I'm not trying to teach you manners at this late date, young man," said Andrews. "I just don't know what you're saying, 'No' to."

"No," stammered Thursty, "we're not all here."

Andrews looked at him, at first blankly, then with concentrated attention.

"What do you mean?"

"I mean Ernst — Ernst Keller. He's at the Battery. At least he was when we left. He was fuf-filling his Mason jar."

Andrews made a rapid calculation. He didn't ask Thursty why he had said nothing at the time. He didn't even remind him that he seemed to have been counted twice when they got into the bus. He just gave Thursty a shriveling look and turned to have a quick word with the teacher who was shepherding the second busload. Then he hopped into a cruising taxi and vanished.

Thursty had seldom been in a Chinese restaurant. Ordinarily he would have liked trying the strange foods, with their different flavors and odd textures. He would certainly have made a point of handling his chopsticks more cleverly than Richy or Peter. He would have enjoyed exploring the spicy-scented Chinese shop afterwards, with its weird drugs that made you think of Oriental mysteries, the gaily colored

dragon kites, the bone figurines, and the jars of long-handled
back-scratchers that made Pete sing out:

> "Hansi, Hansi, do you know
>   Where our doggie got his fleas?
>   Heinie, Heinie, I can't say
>   Because he doesn't sleep with me."

But neither the lunch nor the visit to the shop gave Thursty
real pleasure. He kept seeing the cold hard look on Andrews'
face, and then he remembered the evening visit that Andrews
had paid to The Welcome, and he pictured Andrews telling
Susi about it, if Ernst were lost, or if anything had happened
to him down at the water.

Slowly the bus wove in and out of the unfamiliar streets
on the homeward journey, halting now and then so that the
boys could have a glimpse of some street corner that fame
had touched with a bloody or a gilded finger. Thursty gradually began to feel more comfortable. Ernst, he told himself,
was probably having a swell time knocking about all alone,
and maybe even finding his way to the bird and animal store
to inspect the mice and the lions. And there was always a
cop to help you find your way if you did get mixed up. If
he had only had his kodak, thought Thursty, he would have
liked nothing better than to wander about down there by
himself, taking pictures that would make Richy's look sick.

And then finally the excursion was over, and the boys
piled out of the buses for the last time to go off to their
respective homes. For Thursty it meant returning to Granny's, to be reminded dismally that he wasn't at home. He

didn't want to have to answer Granny's questions as to how he had enjoyed the trip.

But Granny didn't ask anything about it. She had quite forgotten it.

"I've been waiting for you, Dwight," she said interestedly. "I want to hear how our little friend is getting on."

"You mean Ernst?" Thursty mumbled.

"No, no, I mean the little girl, the daughter of that poor man who was picked up for trying to sell his own camera."

"Oh, her," said Thursty, recalling that Marguerite Armand was now under Susi's wing, and wishing privately that Marguerite's father had really been the thief, because then he might have his kodak. "I guess she's all right."

"Didn't Earl tell you anything about her?" pursued Granny.

"Earl? Oh, you meant Ernst. No," said Thursty.

"Well," said Granny, disappointed, for she seemed to feel that the little Marguerite had become her property, "you make sure and ask him about the child tomorrow."

Next morning when it was time for Thursty to go off to school Granny was still sleeping, so she had no chance to remind him about Marguerite. Thursty was too much taken up with the prospect of facing Mr. Andrews and of meeting Ernst again to think of her.

It was disconcerting to discover, at roll call, that Ernst was absent. Andrews volunteered no information, and the morning was not rendered pleasanter by the fact that he required a written report on the excursion. Thursty, trying to review all the places they had visited and the special things they had been told about each one, could recall clearly only the first half of the trip. What they had seen after finally leaving the Battery was a muddle in his mind. He scribbled for a while, and then, at a loss, drew miniature comics on the back of his left hand. But they gave him no particular pleasure.

When the bell rang he marched up to Mr. Andrews and demanded, in a voice that surprisingly suggested that Andrews was himself at fault:

"Did you find Ernst?"

Andrews tapped his pencil deliberately on the desk a minute before answering.

"Yes," he said slowly, "I found him."

"Oh." Thursty was immensely relieved.

"I found him," Andrews went on, "in the river."

It was not merely Andrews' cold voice but the fact that he didn't seem to want to look at Thursty that was chilling. Andrews said nothing further, merely reached for Thursty's blotted half page, and in doing so caught sight of the inky drawing on the back of his hand.

"Nice art work," he commented dryly, "but your report is pretty short. Too bad you can't hand in the illustration."

Thursty reddened. He wanted to ask about Ernst, but he was afraid. Before he could formulate his question the second bell had rung and he had to dash to another classroom.

The day dragged on, one dull lesson after another, and finally luncheon. Thursty hesitated to confide in either Pete or Richy. He might have turned to Booker, for some reason that he himself didn't understand: actually it was because Booker liked Ernst, while Pete and Richy did not, but something put a clamp on his tongue. Luncheon was a gloomy meal, partly because news was going round that the gym period would be killed for the sake of physical examinations. Pete boasted that he had the last line of the eye chart by heart: L E F O D P C T, and began taking bets on the respective weights of Fatty Rossiter and Long John Pringle, stripped. Thursty made his wager with the rest, but though he stood to win a dime on one bet and a week's sodas on another, his heart was not in it. He left the others to their gambling and turned off down the hall.

"Well, Thursty."

It was Mr. Andrews.

"You're not far from The Welcome these days, are you?"

"No," Thursty answered, surprised no less at the question than at the unexpectedly friendly tone in which it was asked.

"How'd you like to step in there on your way home and take Ernst his lessons?"

"Sure, Mr. Andrews!" Thursty said explosively. He didn't know just what he'd been afraid of, but this somehow made everything all right again. Andrews had wanted to scare him. That was his idea of punishing him for having left Ernst in the lurch. Thursty thought old-fashioned punishments had something to be said for them. They couldn't make you any more miserable than this. But he wondered if you felt as good when a licking stopped hurting as he did now.

The rest of the day passed rapidly and pleasantly enough. The rumor about physical examinations proved to be wrong and instead there was a soccer game at which Thursty outdid himself. Pete insisted, however, on hanging on to the pennies and nickels and dimes deposited with him, asserting that there were bound to be physical exams soon, and the bets would hold. He stood firm, even when Richy pointed out that Fatty would have time to consume a number of sodas in the meanwhile and might easily put on weight. The boys were approaching the Soda Shoppe as the discussion came to a conclusion, but for once Thursty resisted its lures. His job was to get down to The Welcome and see Ernst with his own eyes.

When he got there, however, he stood on the doorstep a moment hesitating. Then he straightened his shoulders, shifted his bulging brief case from one hand to the other and turned the doorknob.

The foyer was empty, but he could hear voices upstairs and Tante Tilda came lumbering from the back of the house.

"So-oh," she said, recognizing Thursty with a curt nod of her gray head, and lumbered out again. Thursty was not disturbed. By this time he knew Tante Tilda. But he didn't quite like to go upstairs: he didn't know in just what shape he'd find Ernst, or what Susi would say to him. She might be even madder than Andrews had been.

Slowly he mounted the twisting staircase and paused on the landing. A door opened up above and one of Susi's helpers came out and peered at him. She was a tall blonde young woman who looked like a girls' gym teacher.

"Hello," she said, with an accent like Susi's. "Do you know where the game room is? Second door on the right." And with a wave of her efficient hand she, too, disappeared. She must have mistaken him for one of the foreign boys who came to The Welcome in the afternoons when school was over. Thursty knew where the game room was, but he didn't go in. He went on up the stairs toward Ernst's room.

It was very quiet. But just as he approached it Thursty heard a tremendous sneeze. He knocked on the door.

"Cub id!"

"Hello," said Thursty, diffidently.

Ernst was sitting up in bed, blowing his nose.

"Hello, Thursty!" he cried, as he withdrew from the enveloping folds of a man-size handkerchief. He didn't seem a bit sore.

"Sit dowd," he said. "But don't cub too close or you bight catch it."

Thursty sat down.

"I brought you your lessons," said Thursty.

"Thaks," said Ernst. "I guess I'b stuck here for a while. But, oh, Sursty, it was fide!"

"What was fine?"

"When I was alode dowd there," declared Ernst.

At first Thursty thought maybe he was being sarcastic. It was hard to understand him, too, talking through his nose with an accent besides. But gradually Thursty discovered that Ernst, instead of being angry at having been deserted, was deeply pleased. Perhaps, unlike Andrews, he thought it was an accident. He'd had a chance to explore a bit, and then it had occurred to him that he might get an even richer assortment of animalcules. So he had crept down to a spot in the lee of the Fireboat Station, and emptied his jar preparatory to refilling it more profitably when a shrill whistle scared him so that he tumbled into the water. The whistle was actually intended to warn him away so that he wouldn't fall in, but it worked the wrong way. At any rate, he was fished out and given dry clothes and was just enjoying some sandwiches and a coke provided by his rescuer, a friendly red-faced man from the Department of Docks, when Mr. Andrews came along, awfully upset because Ernst was nowhere in sight when he arrived and the rumor was going about the park that a boy had been drowned that morning. It was a little difficult to explain to Ernst that the trick Thursty had played had not been intended as an act of kindness. Thursty didn't try. And when Susi came in, and in one breath thanked Thursty for coming and reproached Ernst for exposing him to his cold, Thursty knew he couldn't confess. Andrews knew and Andrews despised him for it, and that was enough.

"Well, fella," he muttered, getting up, and swinging his brief case to and fro to ease his embarrassment, "be seeing you."

"So logg, Thursty!" Ernst answered with a farewell sneeze.

Susi took Thursty to the door.

"*Na,* that was quite an adventure Ernst had," she said, smiling.

Thursty began wondering just how much Susi knew about the adventure. Hadn't Andrews said anything when he brought Ernst back?

A door opened above stairs and the strumming of a guitar mingled with the shrill voices of very little children singing some foreign song with a boisterous refrain:

> "*Ri — ra — rutsch!*
> *Wir fahren in dem Kutsch!*"

Thursty was reminded suddenly of Marguerite. But before

he had a chance to ask after her, Susi put a hand on his shoulder and said gently,

"Thursty, I have a favor to ask of you."

"Sure," he answered, wondering what it could be.

"Don't tell Ernst that he was left behind on purpose. He thinks it was an accident. And he did have a lot of fun, even if he caught cold. It will be just a secret between you and me, yes?"

"And Mr. Andrews?" asked Thursty.

"And Mr. Andrews," said Susi in a conspiratorial tone.

"But — " began Thursty.

"Promise?" asked Susi, and though her tone was pleading, there was a twinkle in her golden-green eyes.

"Ri — ra — rutsch!" sounded gleefully from upstairs.

"Sure, I promise," said Thursty.

Susi was a queer one. The Welcome was a queer place. But he was filled with an inexplicable liking for both that included even the betrayed and ignorantly happy Ernst, sneezing away into his big handkerchief. It was only as Thursty turned the corner that he remembered that he had not asked about Marguerite. She must be O.K. though. Thursty swung his brief case vigorously. If he kept on as he had today, he thought, maybe he'd make the Varsity soccer team. There'd be a game tomorrow, sure, if they didn't have those dumb exams. And if they did, why, perhaps he'd win fifty cents on Fatty Rossiter. The rest of the way home he spent wondering cheerfully what Sarah would give him for dinner.

CHAPTER THIRTEEN

Ernst's cold kept him away from school for several days. Every afternoon Thursty went to carry him his lessons. Not out of kindness so much as by way of mild penance for having played the trick on him.

It was during one of Thursty's brief visits that Susi popped in to say that he wasn't the only one with a birthday this season: Ernst and Erica were having a double celebration the following Saturday. If only Ernst were well by then, Susi added anxiously, with a sneeze on her own account.

And here it was Saturday. And Thursty, slightly surprised at himself, was on his way to the party. The first half of it, that is, the luncheon at the Molnars'. And then they were going to The Welcome for the second half.

Thursty wasn't sure that he would like the Molnars: Aunt Frances and Uncle Stephen. They weren't a real aunt and uncle anyway. And they'd behaved pretty shabbily when the twins came, accepting Erica and leaving Ernst out in the cold. Thursty figured that it was much jollier for Ernst at The Welcome than it could be anywhere else, but when the Molnars had palmed him off on Susi they couldn't have known that.

He was reconciled to a luncheon with these strange and probably snooty people by the fact that the food would probably be rather special — Thursty did like to eat! — and that he would have a chance to see the mysterious Erica. Thursty continued to be puzzled by Ernst's eagerness to be with her. Even if she was his twin, she was only a girl. Ever since Silly's measles had put Thursty out of the house, he had been wanting to get home again, but not for Silly's sake.

The Molnars lived in the East Fifties in an old-fashioned brownstone house with a high stoop. Thursty vaguely remembered stories of Moth's childhood associated with just such a house. He supposed it would be like Granny's, full of ancient furniture that you didn't dare jump on and delicate curios you mustn't handle. When the door was opened by a maid in a crisp gray uniform, he saw that he was right.

A slight blonde lady with a pointed face who looked like a friendly fox with bright blue eyes came out and smiled at Thursty. He supposed she was Aunt Frances.

"You must be Dwight Thurston," she said.

Thursty nodded awkwardly.

"Won't you come in," she said then, waving him toward the drawing room, but to his relief not accompanying him. "Ernst and Erica will be down in a moment."

Thursty walked into an immense tapestried room that reminded him of a museum, and sat down gingerly on a fragile chair. Golly, he thought to himself, why didn't the guy who had taken his kodak come to this place? He'd have got really valuable stuff here, and there was so much of it that nobody would have missed things. In spite of the trip the class had taken around the city, he hadn't realized that there were such awfully old houses in New York. Not that people you knew lived in. Ernst was lucky not to have been taken by the Molnars. It was different with a girl.

Thursty began to worry about the luncheon. They'd probably have all kinds of fancy food and nothing really to eat, and he'd get mixed up on the right fork to use, and maybe there'd even be a butler who would fix him with a cold eye and breathe down his neck. He was in the midst of these dismal reflections, his head bent, so that all he saw was a corner of the rich rug near the window, when he noticed that the drapery was moving suspiciously. There was something alive behind that drapery. Thursty watched, fascinated. And as he watched, a tiny creature streaked across the floor, like a whisper, in a flash. And Thursty realized that the mansion held a mouse!

He was familiar with mice. Every summer when they went back to the farm they had to dispossess families of field mice who had occupied the rooms in the Thurstons' absence. But he had never seen what you might call a house mouse. It occurred to him that it was a lucky thing Erica hadn't been present: she would probably have shrieked.

Just then he heard feet on the stairs, and Ernst ran in with Erica behind him. Thursty jumped up and stuck into Ernst's hand the presents he had brought: a Scout knife for Ernst and — with vague thoughts of Silly when he'd bought it — a set of colored pencils for Erica.

"Oh, san — thank you, Thursty!" cried Ernst, delighted.

Thursty eyed Erica, who was slower in unwrapping her box. She was as much like her brother as a girl could be: the same slight-boned figure, the same tobacco-colored hair, the same gray-blue eyes set in a pale oval face. If she had been a boy, thought Thursty, and he were sizing her up for the team, he'd have had her play guard, for all she was so thin. She looked pretty keen.

"Thank you very much," she said politely, as she took out, one after another, the red and the blue and the violet and the yellow pencils. But then she saw Ernst's gift and her eyes sparkled.

"Oh, Ernst!" she breathed.

The heck with it, thought Thursty: she wants the Scout knife.

"Ernst," she repeated, laying her hand on his arm, "you have always need of colored pencils. For drawing. What you see under the microscope at school. But I —"

"But you need a knife?" asked Ernst, grinning in a jolly fashion that was quite novel to Thursty.

"Yes," said Erica happily. "I do. You see, Aunt Frances is very sweet, and Uncle Stephen, he is always trying to give me a good time. But they do not understand. Think: he nearly got me a doll for my birthday!" Erica burst into giggles.

"What would you do with a knife?" asked Ernst.

"What would *you* do?" Erica retorted. "Besides," she went on rapidly, speaking, Thursty noticed, with much less of an accent than Ernst, "if I had a knife, and such a good one, even if I did not use it," she shrugged, "I would feel — more like myself."

Ernst seemed undecided.

"They are beautiful pencils," murmured Erica.

"All right," said Ernst finally. "We trade. If Thursty doesn't mind?" He looked inquiringly at his friend, who shook his head. "But," Ernst went on, "you know why, Erica. It is because I could not buy you a really good present myself. And because, well, somehow, for luck . . ."

Thursty knew what he meant. Ernst really wanted the Scout knife himself, but he felt that if he surrendered it to

Erica in exchange for the pencils, the Powers That Be might arrange it that he'd get let off a trip to the dentist, or score a touchdown, or have whatever it was that he specially wanted.

"Do you like to draw, too, Thursty?" asked Erica, as though she had made the exchange because there was nothing Ernst wanted as badly as the pencils.

That was just like a girl, Thursty reflected. But before he had time to say anything, Erica darted off to another corner of the immense rich room and came back holding in her arms the most magnificent cat Thursty had ever seen. He preferred dogs to cats, of course, but this creature was extraordinary. Her gray fur was so fine and soft and thick that you wanted to plunge your fingers deep into it, but the enormous eyes, like liquid emeralds, held you off. She looked like a half domesticated tigress of an imperial breed, and it was with a kind of royal condescension that she submitted to Erica's caresses.

"This is Baldroulbadour," said Erica, laying her cheek against the cat's side. "She is purring like a grandfather's clock."

Thursty had never heard a grandfather's clock purr, but he knew what Erica meant.

"She's a beauty," he agreed. And then, the words coming out without his wanting them to: "Is she a good mouser?"

"Baldroulbadour!" cried Erica. "When she gets liver, and fish, and sometimes the top of the milk! What would she want with mice?"

"Oh," said Thursty. "But — in a house," he didn't want to say: "an old house," thinking it mightn't be polite, "you sometimes have mice. And they're a nuisance — they eat things. Once on the farm —"

"Do you have a farm?" asked Erica, her indignation changing to sudden warm curiosity. "That is wonderful!"

"Just a very small one," said Thursty modestly.

Erica was all right, he decided, though she jumped from one thing to the next before you knew where you were at. She did it again now.

"I like mice," she said. "I would never catch a mouse. Ernst might. Ernst might even kill it to look at under the microscope . . ." She pouted at her brother.

Ernst laughed.

"I would have to dissect it first —"

"Ugh!" Erica shuddered dramatically, and Baldroul-badour, annoyed by this disregard of her sensibilities, leapt out of Erica's arms.

And then Aunt Frances tripped into the room, and created a diversion by summoning them to luncheon. It was not as bad as Thursty had feared. There was no butler, only a neat waitress, of whom he didn't have to be shy, though he could not imagine anyone being easy with her as he was with Delia at home and Sarah at Granny's, or as Ernst was with gruff Tante Tilda at The Welcome. The food was delicious, and there weren't too many forks. Aunt Frances tried to be very jolly and pleasant. She had a little running laugh that kept interrupting like the coach's whistle at a game. Grown-ups didn't understand that when you were eating you didn't have to talk. Thursty wished, in spite of the thick juicy steak and the baked potatoes puffy with cheese, that luncheon would be over soon, so that they could go on down to Susi's.

"Yes," Aunt Frances said, breaking a silence that Thursty found quite satisfactory, "you do grow up ever so fast. I can't believe that these are the two babies whom we used to take to the *Konditorei* for *Schokolade* with *Schlagsahne* (that's chocolate with whipped cream)," she explained to Thursty. Her voice trailed off, and then she resumed briskly:

"Uncle Stephen used to call you 'kiddies,' and once, Ernst, you asked what it meant, and Uncle Stephen said kids were little goats, but Ernst said, 'I am not a little goat, I am a fireman!' " Aunt Frances laughed again. Thursty didn't think it was so funny. He had wanted to be a fireman once too, when he was a baby. "And the fireman was going to marry Susi when he grew up! Do you remember?" asked Aunt Frances.

It was as though she were cross with Ernst about it, though she smiled as she spoke.

"And Erica," Aunt Frances went on, without waiting for an answer, "used to wheel the dachshund around in her doll carriage. I suppose," she added, apologetically, "that's why Uncle Stephen wanted to give you a doll for your birthday, Erica. He was remembering the dachshund. What was his name?"

"Knirps," said Ernst and Erica in one voice.

"Knirps," repeated Aunt Frances. "I'm afraid you'd never get Baldroulbadour to consent to such treatment." She turned to Thursty. "Have you seen Baldroulbadour?"

"Yeah," mumbled Thursty, his mouth full of frozen pudding, and gulped it down hastily at a smothered shriek from the pantry. A moment later Baldroulbadour in person emerged from behind the screen, to pad lightly across the floor, something hanging from her mouth.

Aunt Frances leapt up, clutching her skirts to her knees, her face screwed up in dismay. Ernst, his spoon suspended in mid-air, and Thursty, openmouthed, pushed back their chairs. But it was Erica who dashed from the table down the long dining room after the cat. She caught her just as Baldroulbadour was about to slip into the hall. With a sudden jerk she pried open Baldroulbadour's jaws, and released the tiny victim. The mouse lay there. If it was alive, it was too terrified to stir. "You bad, wicked cat!" Erica sobbed. She looked as if she were going to beat the cat. The magnificent Persian crouched — was it in tigerish fury or self-defense? — staring at Erica out of cold emerald eyes, and then, like an outraged queen, rose up and stalked away. When Thursty looked for the mouse, it was gone.

"Erica!" cried Aunt Frances, with a shiver of distaste. "How could you?"

"Erica," said Ernst breathlessly, "she might have scratched out your eyes!"

"Gee!" said Thursty, "that was something!"

But Erica merely got up from her knees, rubbed her eyes hastily with the back of her hand and said in a husky voice: "I'm glad it got away!"

"But if it had been dead," murmured Ernst thoughtfully, "I could have used it better than Baldroulbadour."

"Dissected it, you mean?" Erica turned on him. "Ernst, you are horrid!"

"Oh, Ernst." Aunt Frances put an arm around Erica, as

though to protect her from that cold savage, her scientifically-minded brother.

"Well," Ernst retorted defensively, looking at Erica, "it is what Pappi does."

"Oh, but Ernst," said Aunt Frances, "that's different. And besides —"

At the mention of her father, Erica moved away from Aunt Frances.

"Maybe you are right," she said. "If the poor little thing had been dead already. Still," she tossed her head, "I'm glad it got away."

There was a moment's awkward silence, broken by Aunt Frances, her voice high with a note of forced cheer.

"Come," she said, "Erica dear, run and wash your hands. You might at least finish your desserts, all of you. Even if it isn't birthday cake." She gave another little laugh, turning apologetically to Thursty: "They seemed to think they had to have their cake at Susi's."

Something in her tone seemed vaguely to imply a reflection on the cake that Susi would provide. Thursty couldn't find words for it, but he felt somehow that Aunt Frances was jealous of Susi.

"I'm not hungry," said Erica.

"But you must wash," Aunt Frances insisted, with the memory of the mouse in her voice.

"We will have something to tell Susi about this party," Ernst said with satisfaction, as Erica left the room.

"I hope it is all right for you to take Erica down there," murmured Aunt Frances anxiously. "You just over that bad

"You bad, wicked cat!" Erica sobbed

cold, and you say Susi had one too. The germs must be all over the place."

Ernst frowned, lisping in his impatience.

"It is nossing. Only one little girl caught it from Susi: ze little Marguerite. You remember, Sursty? And she," he added, "is staying home."

"Marguerite Armand, the thief's daughter?" asked Thursty.

"Ze painter's daughter," Ernst corrected him quickly, as Aunt Frances stared.

"Sure, I know. He wasn't a real thief," Thursty explained to her carefully. "That was the cop's mistake. And the kid isn't there anyway," he rattled on hastily.

He was just beginning to wonder if they would ever get down to Susi's, when Erica returned, and just after her there entered a tall man, all in brown, from his highly polished shoes to his short mustache and darting eyes. He would have been handsome if he hadn't looked so much like an advertisement in a smart magazine. Uncle Stephen.

"Hello, everybody!" he said gaily, kissing Aunt Frances lightly on the top of her blonde hair, and patting Ernst's shoulder.

"Well, Ernst, how does it feel to be thirteen?" he asked, and without waiting for an answer, he turned his smile on Thursty like an inquiring flashlight.

Thursty was relieved when the introductions were over. But then Uncle Stephen had to hear all about Erica's rescuing the mouse from Baldroulbadour.

"Not very nice of Baldroulbadour," commented Uncle Stephen. "We give her such civilized food and she goes savage on us like that." But though he laughed about it, you could see that he approved neither of the cat nor of Erica, suggesting that Baldroulbadour hadn't behaved as a dignified Persian, nor Erica as a proper little girl should.

He didn't, however, agree with Aunt Frances that Erica should give up the plan of going down with Ernst and Thursty to finish the celebration at Susi's. On the contrary, he volunteered to drive them across town.

Thursty had no idea what would greet them at The Welcome. But he was fairly sure that it would be jollier than this.

CHAPTER FOURTEEN

During the short trip neither of the twins had anything to say. It was enlivened for Thursty by the discovery that Uncle Stephen was an enthusiastic amateur photographer, who went in for color films and had made miles of movies. If Ernst had cared about cameras instead of his old microscope, what a whale of a time he might have had!

When they pulled up in front of the blue door, however, Uncle Stephen seemed to change character. He sent many polite messages to Susi, but refused to come in, and he was quite firm about calling for Erica promptly at six. Above all, he insisted on repeating the various warnings Aunt Frances had given her when they started out — almost as though The Welcome were a contagious hospital.

What it was really like, Thursty found, once he got inside, was the school corridors just before a big game or a festival. Boys and girls, little and big, were spilling out of the rooms into the halls and onto the narrow staircase. It was noisy and confused and jolly, and there was a sound of a guitar from one room and of hammers from below stairs.

It was queer, the way The Welcome seemed to change people. Just approaching the door had stiffened Uncle Stephen as if he had swallowed a poker, while as soon as they entered, Erica had dropped the good-little-girl air she had worn so silently on the way over, and, throwing her arms around Ernst, had given him a violent bear-hug. Ernst submitted, flushing, and asking as soon as he was released,

"Don't you want to see Susi?"

"I want to see Tante Tilda first," cried Erica, making for the kitchen.

But at that moment Susi appeared, waving a dish towel like a banner and calling out:

"*Na,* there you are at last! But you mustn't go into the kitchen, my *Kinderle.* Tante Tilda would never forgive me if I let you peek now."

"Is it a surprise, Susi?" asked Erica eagerly, as though it could be anything else! "Oh, Susi, is it —"

"Ssh!" whispered Susi. "You will see. But first you want to visit Ernst's room, no? And you, Thursty," she said, "you have never been here on a Saturday. It is a nice madhouse then. Everybody comes, because there is no school. Only little Marguerite, you remember her, Thursty, you sent her to us — she is home in bed with a bad cold. I would not mind so much, but the poor little thing has to stay all alone at the top of the house: her mother is out working, and now her father too."

Thursty felt that in a way he was responsible for Marguerite's cold, but at the same time he knew that Susi knew it was thanks to him that Marguerite had come to The Welcome.

"One of us always runs over to see her at lunchtime: the lodginghouse is just around the corner," Susi explained. The wrinkle in her forehead meant that it was a cheap lodginghouse and a horrid cramped little room. But at once she smiled and said quickly: "I am so glad you are here, Thursty! Tante Tilda won't have the twins in the kitchen because she made for them something special." She paused briefly, and whispered: "A *Himmeltorte*!" From Susi's expression Thursty guessed that this must taste like the kind of cake that could only be made in Heaven. "*You* can go in, though, Thursty," Susi added, "and you can help me to start the games. We must fetch the big tub of water for apple-bobbing, and the sacks for the potato race, yes?"

Those were kid games, thought Thursty, but the glint in Susi's golden-green eyes and the laughter in her brisk voice acknowledged that the pair of them knew it and could manage to have fun anyway.

Susi went into the kitchen with him. Tante Tilda, looking like a gray witch, was stirring something thick and fragrant in a bowl and muttering to herself. Susi dragged out a big preserving kettle and stood looking at it quizzically, while Tante Tilda stared at her as though she had gone quietly mad.

"Why don't we fill it, Susi?" Thursty wanted to know.

"We can't possibly carry it upstairs, once it's full of water," said Susi, "strong as you are, Thursty. And there's no room to play anywhere else."

"Tell you what," suggested Thursty, "we'll carry it up empty, and then we'll fill it by pitcherfuls, in a kind of relay: there are enough kids to have it go fast. It'll be like putting out a fire without a hose!"

Susi clapped her hands with delight, as though she couldn't have thought of it herself.

"Wonderful, Thursty! They'll love it. But I must get the bigger ones to do it, the small ones will spill the water all over. Go down to the basement, yes, and fetch some boys from the shop."

So Thursty trotted downstairs to the room from which

the hammering and sawing was sounding. He felt efficient and executive. And when he got there, whom should he find directing the sawing and hammering but Mr. Andrews, in his shirt sleeves.

In a jiffy half a dozen boys, and Mr. Andrews himself, were passing pitchers of water from hand to hand, out of the kitchen into the foyer up the stairs, full and dripping jugs going up, the empties coming down. The tub was filled all too soon. But then they insisted on using the same system for transporting the apples they were to duck for, the potatoes they were to race with, and the sacks they were to wear in the race. It was almost disappointing when the jobs were done and the games could really begin.

But even the games had their points of interest. There was the boy who ducked for apples so boldly that he ducked himself too. And there was the other boy in the donkey game who pinned the donkey's tail on the back of Mr. Andrews. And it was Mr. Andrews who had blindfolded him. And then there was the little dumb girl — she wasn't really dumb, but she was quite new, and spoke a language that even Susi didn't understand. Susi said she didn't know a word of English. She hobbled and bumped across the floor in the potato race with a determination that was wonderful to witness. And she came in even ahead of Erica, who was bigger and awfully good at it besides. The remarkable part was that when she won, and Susi presented her with the prize, which was a very small doll in a very pink dress, she said, in plain English: "Thank you! Oh, I like her! I call her Susi, for you. Susi Welcome!"

Susi chuckled appreciatively over the compliment and gave

the child a quick hug. And then Tante Tilda summoned her, and she came back to announce that it was time to eat.

So they all trooped downstairs, Ernst and Erica coming at the tail of the procession, so that they could be greeted on their entrance to the dining room by an assortment of voices of both sexes and various ages and accents, chorusing unevenly but gaily: "Happy Birthday to you, happy birthday to you, happy birthday, dear Ernst'n'Erica, happy birthday to YOU!"

Thursty liked all of it, even to the two thrones that Susi had decorated, one at the head and one at the foot of the long table, with autumn leaves and evergreens, for each of the twins. It wasn't just because Erica was transported at the sight, and Ernst got red-faced and shiny-eyed. It took ever so little to get them excited. What pleased Thursty was that Ernst and Erica nearly had a fight over which of the two Thursty should sit beside.

"Guess we'll have to cut Thursty in half," drawled Mr. Andrews, with a wink at Susi, with whom he seemed to be on wonderfully friendly terms.

"*Na,*" said Susi. "Ernst, you have him every day. Today is Erica's turn."

So Thursty had the place of honor on Erica's right hand, and though he would have preferred sitting next to her brother, he felt properly proud at being fought over. At any rate, he had proved to Andrews that Ernst held nothing against him. Tante Tilda came and stood in the doorway a moment, arms akimbo, and actually smiled. And Susi hovered about the table, seeing that the smaller ones had sufficiently tall chairs and pointing out the more interesting sandwiches to the older ones.

Thursty was wondering how soon the famous *Himmeltorte* would be brought in, and what it would taste like, when he heard a noise above the buzz of voices and clink of glass and china. It was a fire engine, and by the clamor, it almost seemed as if the fire were next door.

A little Spanish boy, to whom fire engines still meant air raids, climbed hastily out of his chair and under the table, trying to pull his neighbor with him. Susi hurried to the rescue. Mr. Andrews ran upstairs to see what could be seen. Thursty would have liked to run with him, but it was plain that Susi counted on him to help keep the company in order, and besides, there was the imminence of the *Himmeltorte*.

In a moment Mr. Andrews came back.

"It seems to be on the southwest corner of the next block," he told Susi. "I could see the smoke even from the front."

Just then Tante Tilda proudly bore the *Himmeltorte* into the dining room. The snowy-peaked edifice with candles glowing brought a chorus of "Oh's" and "Ah's." As Tante Tilda stood there, holding the festive cake, the excitement stirred by the fire engines was momentarily forgotten. Erica, wriggling on her leafy throne, cried out in delight. The little Spaniard stood clutching Susi's hand, his flushed cheeks still stained with tears, his great dark eyes fixed on the candlelit tart as though that were proof of safety.

"Set it in front of Erica," Susi told Tante Tilda softly, her own eyes beaming, her warm cheeks dimpling with pleasure, as she glanced from Erica to Mr. Andrews in that way grownups have. "Slice it carefully, Erica. But first, you must wish on the candles."

Erica stood up and shut her eyes. She looked as though her wish were something tremendous. Thursty glanced down the table toward Ernst. But Ernst wasn't there!

Susi must have looked for him at the same moment, for she cried out in a low voice,

"*Na,* where is he?" and then quickly bent over the little Spaniard, and, murmuring reassurances, led him to his seat.

Erica opened her eyes and said:

"Now, Ernst, you wish. Then it must come true!" And at once she too cried out: "But where is he?"

"I'll see," said Susi quietly. "He must have gone to the kitchen for something."

It was plain that he couldn't have left the dining room any other way, because then Mr. Andrews would have noticed him. It was all very mysterious. The candles on the cake were burning down. That was just like Ernst, thought Thursty, always not there. Thursty was eager to get away to see the fire. And if he couldn't do that, he did want a mouthful of *Himmeltorte.*

Susi came back immediately.

"I can't find him," she said. "I suspect he ran out the back way." She turned to Erica with an encouraging smile. "I guess Ernst's wish was to see the fire. Never mind, Erica: your wish was strong enough for both," she said, as if it were really important. "Now blow out the candles and start cutting. Ernst will have his slice when he gets back."

"You can't have your fire and eat it too," said Thursty, getting his proverb a little mixed, but hoping that Erica understood that it was meant as a reproof to Ernst for having kept them waiting.

Erica looked anxious but took up the cake knife.

"Take out the candles first," Susi warned her.

"Yes, of course." Erica put the knife down again, and began removing the candles, her lips pursed as she tried to do so without spoiling the frosting. You could tell that she was annoyed with her brother for his curious behavior.

She had just taken out the last candle and was delicately licking a bit of frosting off her finger when there was a terrific bang of the front door and a noise of voices and hurried footsteps on the stairs.

"Quiet," said Susi firmly, turning to face the door. *"Gott im Himmel!"* she said under her breath.

It was Ernst, his face smudged like a coal heaver's, his eyelids red, his hair and clothes rumpled. Behind him was M. Armand, carrying a charred and slightly damp blanket out of which peeped the pale face of the little Marguerite. The entrance of the strange trio was the signal for the small Spaniard to begin wailing, and Erica, the cake knife in her hand, jumped up crying,

"Ernst! Are you hurt? Ernst!"

It was Susi who captured the knife, so that Ernst should not be fatally injured, and it was Mr. Andrews who felt him all over to make sure there were no bones broken, but it was Tante Tilda who, in an ecstasy of grumbling, got Marguerite swiftly and safely into bed, with a piece of *Himmeltorte* to eat after she had swallowed her hot milk, and the little Spaniard to sit beside her with a cheering slice for himself. And on the other side of the bed the dumb girl who had burst so

surprisingly into English speech, tried to make up her mind
whether or not to offer Marguerite the loan of "Susi Welcome." And at the foot of the bed stood M. Armand, looking
at once bewildered and relieved.

In the bathroom, between soapings and splashings, Ernst
explained to Thursty what had happened.

He had slipped out at the back entrance, as Susi suspected.
It wasn't, though, just for the excitement of watching the
fire. He had suddenly realized that the burning house was the
one in which the Armands lodged, and that little Marguerite
was alone in bed on the top floor. He had rushed over to see
that when she was found she should be taken to Susi's. But
when he got there, he discovered that nobody knew anything
about the child. Ernst had tried to fight his way up the smoky
stairs to get to her and been snatched away with nothing
worse than smarting eyes and singed hair to show for it. But
even if he hadn't carried Marguerite out bodily, he had been
responsible for her rescue. M. Armand, coming home early
from work, had found Ernst trying to persuade the fireman
who held his child to carry her to Susi's. And so the fireman
handed her over to her father, in the blanket singed by the
flames and wet by the hose, and the three, M. Armand, Marguerite, and a sooty but triumphant Ernst, had made their
way to The Welcome.

When Ernst was finally cleaned up the exodus had begun.
Already Uncle Stephen was on hand to take Erica home.

Thursty understood her reluctance to go. He didn't particularly want to go back to Granny's himself.

"You'd think," he said to Ernst, "that a birthday would

be enough by itself, but when Something New is Added —
whew! I had a burglary and you two had a fire."

"A fire's better," said Erica firmly.

"I guess you're right," Thursty admitted. "It's more like
Fourth of July."

"But oh, Ernst," said Erica, "you didn't wish on the
candles."

Ernst smiled.

"No, but," said Erica, "you know what I wished. I can't
say, because that might spoil it, but — oh, Ernst, you should
have wished it too!"

"I know," said Ernst, looking serious.

"Well, Erica," interrupted Uncle Stephen, "aren't you
ever coming home, my dear?"

"Home?" Erica repeated tonelessly.

"Yes," said Uncle Stephen, "you'll have plenty to tell
Aunt Frances, eh?"

Erica nodded.

"Good-by, Ernst," she said in a low voice. "Good-by,
Thursty."

"Good-by," said Thursty. " 'By, Ernie," he added. For
he must leave, too.

As he trotted slowly toward Granny's he wondered what
it was that Erica could have wished for so hard and so super-
stitiously. And then he forgot about it, thinking over the
events of the afternoon. Granny would be sure to ask him
what had happened, but there was just too much to tell.

To his surprise and somewhat to his disappointment, however, Granny didn't ask him anything. She didn't even scold

him for being late. Instead, she looked at him sharply and announced:

"I've some news for you, Dwight."

Thursty's heart quickened so that he could feel it beating. The kodak — it had been returned!

"Well?" said Granny. "Don't you want to hear it?"

"Sure," said Thursty. "What is it?"

"Your mother just telephoned. You can go home tomorrow."

Thursty felt a prick of disappointment, but it was immediately swallowed up in joy. Home!

"Oh, boy!" he breathed. And began suddenly doing a rapid tap dance.

"What's got into you?" demanded Sarah, watching him without enthusiasm. "You so glad to leave us?"

"Course no," said Thursty impatiently. "But don't you get it? I'm going home!"

CHAPTER FIFTEEN

Being at home again was the jolliest thing that had happened to Thursty since he had received his ill-fated kodak on his birthday morning. It was good to see Moth' again. It was fun to sneak down cellar secretly with Pop to see the work he'd started on the doll house that was to be Silly's Christmas present. Going into the kitchen to tease Delia about the Sunday dinner was a pleasure Thursty hadn't tasted in weeks. He didn't even mind Silly, for once. She was cuter, he discovered, than any of the kids at The Welcome, even if she did screw up her eyes and wriggle the tip of her nose like a rabbit when she wanted attention.

Thursty went into his own room and looked everything over with fresh interest. He turned on his radio. It was just a set of naked tubes, because it had been knocked down once in a scuffle and the plastic box had broken to bits. But he liked it better than Granny's Capehart. There were only sermons on at the moment, but he rejoiced in the thought that later on he could listen to whatever bloodcurdling mystery he chose without having to consult anybody else.

He stood contemplating the low bookcase with the cracked glass doors that formed his museum. It had really curious things in it, that you didn't need the help of a microscope to see, like the stinky pond water Ernst guarded so carefully. There was the jawbone of a horse that was maybe prehistoric, or anyway awfully old, and a snake's rattles, and some fossils that Thursty had found himself, and a dusty wasp's nest like a gray paper skull. Then there was a set of odd coins. And three tiny bottles that had once held samples of wine. Silly was always begging him for those bottles to play house with, as though dolls would drink wine! — and he was afraid that while he'd been gone, Pop might have let her have the loan of them. You could never tell how he'd spoil the kid next. But there they were safe and sound. And on the wall opposite was the picture of a kangaroo he'd painted last year. He had a baby kanga sticking out of its pouch, and over it a sign in block capitals: BEWARE OF PICKPOCKETS! It was neat. It was funny, but it was always easier to paint or draw animals that you didn't see every day, like kangaroos and elephants, rather than cats and dogs. Why were the creatures with interesting shapes all foreign ones, he wondered.

There was a special cache in the bookcase, on the bottom shelf behind the dictionary and the big atlas, where he kept refreshments for the times when Delia was washing the kitchen floor and wouldn't let him in. He wondered if he would find something there now. He had just put his hand on the atlas when he heard small steps behind him and there was Silly, saying:

"Come and have din-din."

Hastily Thursty withdrew his exploring fingers.

"Don't say 'din-din,' Silly. It's dinNER!" he said in a severe voice that was to prevent her from asking what he was doing. Silly mustn't ever discover the box of crackers or the half empty jar of sweet pickles that might be nestling behind those books.

"DinNER," repeated Silly, so obediently that Thursty swung her up behind him, and carried her off to the dining

room pickaback. When she chanted, "Piggyback, piggyback!" in the conviction that this was the way pigs were
taken to market, he didn't even correct her.

It would be nice, though, he thought, as he dumped her
down, if Silly were his twin.

"Well, Dwight," Pop grinned at him across the loaded
table, "how does it feel to be home?"

"Swell!" said Thursty.

And suddenly in a kind of flashback he remembered that
moment last evening at The Welcome when Uncle Stephen
had turned to Erica and said, "Aren't you ever coming home,
my dear?" and she had repeated, "Home?"

Thursty went after the noodles in his soup plate almost
savagely. It wasn't so much that he was sorry for Erica and
for Ernst, who couldn't look forward to a real homecoming,
or sorry for little Marguerite Armand, tucked away on a
couch at The Welcome to recover from her fright and exposure after the fire. Thursty was sorry for himself, having to
remember those kids just when he wanted to think of nothing
but Sunday dinner with the family.

Delia brought in the roast chicken.

"I want the wishbone," piped up Silly.

"It won't be much of a one," said Pop as he took up the
carving knife. "You'll have to wait for Thanksgiving for
one worth wishing on."

"Yes, and it's almost here," said Moth', with a little sigh.

Grownups never looked forward to holidays properly,
thought Thursty. And yet they seemed to have just as good
a time as anybody when the occasion arrived. And they never
had to go to bed just when things were getting interesting.

"Will we go to the farm for Thanksgiving this year?" he asked.

"Sure thing," said Pop.

"Goody, goody, goody!" cried Silly, nearly turning her chair over in her rejoicing.

She was slower than Thursty in settling down to the real business of dinner. As usual, she tried to eat her peas without touching her carrots.

"Look," she said, before she was half way through, "is the wishbone dry enough now?"

Thursty examined it critically.

"Not quite."

"Oh, I want to wish," said Silly plaintively. "I wish —"

And again Thursty was carried back to yesterday, when Erica had wished on the birthday candles.

"Don't tell," he warned Silly, "or it won't come true!"

Silly, clutching the bone tightly in her tiny fingers, stared at him wide-eyed, on the verge of tears.

"But," she stammered, "I'm wishing that it was Thanksgiving. Does that mean it won't be Thanksgiving ever?"

At which prospect her tears spilled over, and everybody laughed, and Pop had to take her on his knee to comfort her.

"It seems a pity," said Moth', "to go up and celebrate with nobody but the four of us and Granny."

"I could ask Pete or Richy," said Thursty. "Trouble is," he added, "they always want to have dinner with their own dear fambilies."

"What's 'fambilies'?" asked Silly.

"That's Kipling," explained Thursty.

"What's kippling? Teach me to kipple," pleaded Silly.

"What can you do with a kid like that?" Thursty asked helplessly, thinking again how different it would be if Silly were his twin.

"We could ask Ernie," he said. "And maybe Erica?" he added. He would have to keep Ernst from falling into the pond in search of specimens, and he didn't know exactly how Erica would fit in. But it was bound to be all right. Suddenly Thanksgiving did seem awfully far away.

But time, that elastic substance, which stretches and shrinks in such incredible ways, collapsed into itself, as it were. And what had seemed so remote was all at once in danger of flashing past without being truly realized.

For here it was, the day before the feast itself.

There had never been such a trip up to the farm as this one, on the Wednesday afternoon, with seven people packed into a five-seater car, that was stuffed like a veritable turkey with special provisions, not to mention the various suitcases, and small extras like Granny's electric pad and Thursty's skis. Pop drove, with Thursty and Ernst squeezed beside him, and Moth' did a little mild back-seat driving, in between begging Granny to sit back more comfortably and telling Silly to stop wriggling and trying, gently and vainly, to draw out the silent Erica.

The last mile or two was a bit trying, for everybody was stiff, Granny and Silly were both cranky, and there was the bad stretch of road through the woods that always made Pop say things in Spanish which he refused to translate. But at last they came to the clearing where the house stood, low-roofed, small, but friendly.

They had no sooner piled themselves and the luggage out

of the car than work began in earnest. Thursty and Ernst had to fetch more firewood. Erica and Moth' began a big job of bedmaking. Pop went for ice, and Granny and Silly sat peaceably on either side of the kitchen stove shelling peas. Delia had prepared as much as she could ahead for them, so that there would be almost nothing to do about next day's dinner but eat it. Yet with seven people to feed over the week end, there was bound to be some unfinished business. The peas were part of it.

Supper was early, and included fresh milk and new-laid eggs that Thursty and Ernst had walked two miles to fetch. Because, as Thursty had to explain to a disappointed Erica, the farm was so called only by courtesy. All that was left of the old place was the remodeled farmhouse, the orchard, and a small kitchen garden. Erica had looked forward to taking care of livestock. Thursty told her that the livestock consisted of stray field mice and, occasionally and most regrettably, ants.

His discouraging words made it all the more wonderful when Erica, who had a cot on the sleeping porch, wakened in the gray hour before dawn to see, like a picture out of the *Jungle Book*, a live deer. It stood in the road a moment, with head lifted inquiringly, and then, as though dissatisfied with the answer to its unvoiced question, it vanished. Erica told them all about it at breakfast with great excitement. Thursty could only think what a marvelous photograph it would have made. But then the hour before the dawn wasn't exactly the best one for photography. And he didn't have his kodak.

What with breakfast to get, to eat, and to wash up after, and more fuel to fetch — Thursty said the stoves all had tapeworm, they ate so much wood — and another trip for milk and eggs, not to mention the preparations for the afternoon feast which engaged all the womenfolk, down to little Silly who had to help set the table, the morning finally wore away.

"There's a story John Mandeville tells," said Pop, sniffing audibly as he helped Ernst dump a load of firewood into the kitchen bin, "about a set of savages who lived on the smell of roast meat. Is that what you expect of us?"

"You'll have to live on smells for just another ten minutes," Moth' answered with a laugh. "In fact, you might as well start washing up for dinner right now."

"Boy, am I hungry!" cried Thursty. "Line forms on the right," he added, as he dashed for the bathroom, which needed as much nursing as the stoves, for water had to be pumped regularly for the old-fashioned tub and the washbowls. Somehow, Thursty didn't mind that, and he rather liked splashing about in the china bowl with the florid roses (or were they red cabbages?). You could really see how much dirt came off.

And finally, there they were, slightly damp but clean, and assured that the delicious odors were only a prelude to the most satisfying mouthfuls. Moth' never bothered with preliminaries like fruit cup or soup on Thanksgiving Day. If you couldn't be content with turkey and trimmings and dessert, she said, she wouldn't give a thank-you for you. Thursty, eyeing the bowls of buttery succotash, peas, and beans, the mounds of cranberry jelly like shivering rubies in which small topaz spheres of apple were set, the relishes sweet and sour, the rich yellow potatoes roofed with toasted marshmallows, all lorded over by the great golden brown bird, and waiting on the pantry shelves the juicy crusty spicy pies, the heaping bowl of apples, nuts and raisins that were to follow — Thursty agreed.

"Say, Ernie," he said, as he gave the Lazy Susan a gentle push, "remember when we were painting the map of the U. S. the beginning of the year, and you asked me, 'What's Thanksgiving?'"

"Yes," said Ernst with a brief smile. "You thought I was a big dope, no?"

"Maybe," Thursty conceded. "Well, this is it."

"It is something that once you have seen you could never forget," Ernst admitted.

"It takes more than seeing," said Thursty, helping himself generously to sweet potatoes. "Before I get through I have to loosen my belt three holes." He glanced sideways at Erica. What did girls do, without belts to loosen?

It was at the tail end of the feast, when everybody had eaten a little more than he thought he could, and Thursty had reluctantly refused a second helping of apple pie, that Pop said with a quizzical grin:

"The Pilgrim Fathers knew what they were celebrating. But I'd like to know what you fellows are chiefly thankful for."

"I'm thankful that I brought my soda mints," said Granny quickly. "And the rest of you should be thankful you don't need 'em."

"I'm thankful for a good deal more than that," said Moth', looking around at them, as Pop had done, with a different kind of smile, meaning plainly enough that she was glad they were all there. She didn't say it, though.

"I'm thankful there's no school till Monday," said Thursty with a sigh of repletion. "How about you, Ernie?"

"Yes," said Ernst, "but —"

"You wouldn't *rather* be at school?" asked Thursty.

"No," said Ernst, his face clouding, "I'd *rather* be —" He didn't finish, and Pop interrupted briskly,

"Well, Silly-girl, how about you?"

"I'm gladdest I haven't got the measles," said Silly.

Erica looked at Pop with a funny little smile.

"What's yours?" she asked.

"You make it sound like a drink," said Pop. "Well, I guess we get a pretty good kick out of the things we're grateful for. Unless they're soda mints," he observed with a wink for Granny. "What's mine?" he repeated thoughtfully. "It's being able to speak my mind, without being afraid of the Big Bad Wolf."

"Who's afraid of the Big Bad Wolf, Big Bad Wolf, Big Bad Wolf?" chanted Thursty, Silly's voice trailing weakly and funnily behind his.

"Isn't there a song we all know?" asked Moth', that being the way she always liked to end up.

It took quite a little research to discover one. Pop suggested the "Pilgrim's Chorus" from *Tannhäuser,* but that was only a bad joke, and Silly wanted "Rum-tum-tiddle-um-tum" from *Winnie the Pooh,* while Granny said the only song everybody knew was the National Anthem. But then it appeared that she meant not the "Star Spangled Banner," but

"My Country 'Tis of Thee." Thursty was just thinking privately how queer it would be for Ernst and Erica to sing the verse about "Land where my fathers died," when they tried to fit the words of "God Save the King" to the tune, which was quite confusing. Moth' finally asked Erica what she would like to sing, and declared that that would have to settle it. Erica plumped for "*Malbrough s'en va-t-en guerre.*" Thursty didn't remember the words very well, but he sang, "We don't go home until morning," instead. Silly asked, "Tomorrow morning?" with a note of sorrow in her small voice, but was reassured and joined in with the rest.

They were in the midst of the chorus, Granny's high quaver set off by Pop's resonant if uncertain bass, when they were interrupted by the sound of an approaching car.

Unexpected visitors were rare at the farm. On Thanksgiving Day they were altogether extraordinary. But what was most astonishing was that they turned out to be Susi and Mr. Andrews.

After the first exclamations were over, and the visitors had confessed that they had already dined, and refused all the good things Moth' offered them except another cup of coffee and another piece of pie, Susi explained that she was in the midst of an adventure.

She had decided that she must have some sort of place that she could turn into a summer "Welcome." She hadn't any money with which to buy one, even a heavily mortgaged one. But Mr. Andrews had persuaded her that this was the time to scout about, and he had offered to take her in his wheezy Ford. And so there they were.

"Oh, if only we could have a place like this!" sighed Susi,

crying out with pleasure over every part of the kitchen, which was also the dining room.

For a moment Thursty was almost afraid Pop was going to turn it over to her.

And then Mr. Andrews began talking about the chicken farm he hoped to own some day.

"You ought to combine the two places," said Moth'. "Maybe then you'd really find something."

"That's an idea!" said Mr. Andrews.

And Susi's warm color got higher than usual, and she was suddenly reminded that they had to get back. They had arrived by most devious ways, and it would take them ever so long to find their way home. So Pop explained about short cuts, and they had to stay a little longer.

But finally the time came when they really had to go. And then Susi, whose arrival made the party seem even gayer than before, spoiled things for Thursty by announcing that Ernst and Erica couldn't, as they'd planned, stay over the whole week end. Because both of them had to be in New York on Sunday.

No amount of pleading would move her to discuss the reason. All she would say was that it was a "good" one in every sense of the word.

CHAPTER SIXTEEN

It was the curse of holidays that the better they were, the sooner they were over. Then you were back on the old treadmill of math and history and English, with only short intervals of relief, like lunch. Except for a football game to look forward to at the close of the day, there was no cause for cheer. But sorrow's crown of sorrow was that every member of the Form had to write a composition on How I Spent My Vacation.

The announcement was greeted by a chorus of groans.

"Just pick out the highlights," said Andrews, pacing slowly up and down the front of the room, and coming to a halt before Thursty's desk. "What you fellows don't seem to get," he added, "is that every time I give you homework, I have twenty times as much homework to do myself. Your stuff has to be corrected. And that means I've got to read it. Ever think of that?"

You wouldn't *have* to give us homework, thought Thursty gloomily. And you know darn well how I spent my vacation.

What'll I say? Thursty asked himself. "So we finished dinner, and then a car drove up. And in it was Mr. Andrews and Susi." Half the fellows won't know who Susi is. They'll think she's Andrews' girl friend. Maybe she is, thought Thursty, puzzled at this new notion and slightly disturbed. Because if she was, and if they actually got married, and Andrews left school to start a chicken farm — what would happen to The Welcome? And to Ernst?

His meditations were cut short by Mr. Andrews, saying:

"I'm going around the room quickly and ask each one of you what the best part of his holiday was. That may give the fellows who think they have nothing to write about some ideas. Jimmy, what's your story?"

Jim Clark didn't hesitate.

"It was the big game in the Yale Bowl."

The class hummed with an envious thrill.

"That's swell! Booker?"

"Guess it was being a super at the Opera."

"Well, that's something!" exclaimed Mr. Andrews. "What did you sing?"

"Oh, no, sir, I didn't sing!" said Booker, with a slow head-shake and a grin. "I just had to stand there, all dressed up and full of grease paint. But, boy, did I hear music!"

Thursty was less impressed by the music than by the notion of Booker on a real stage, rubbing shoulders with real stars. Nobody could match that.

Mr. Andrews called on one after another. Fatty Rossiter could think of nothing more interesting than his Thanksgiving dinner. Richy had gone to a super-duper movie, and Pete mentioned an afternoon he'd spent at The Gay Blades learning some fancy turns on skates from a pro. For all Pete appeared so superior about it, Thursty preferred the pond at the farm, when it froze thick enough.

In a moment it would be Ernst's turn to speak. Thursty hoped he'd say something about the farm. And suddenly he recalled the surprise that Susi had had up her sleeve, for the sake of which Ernst and Erica had missed Sunday in the country. Thursty hadn't yet learned what it was all about.

"Well, Ernst," said Mr. Andrews, smiling, "what was the best part of your vacation?"

"Broadcasting," answered Ernst.

The class stared.

"Better say where to," suggested Andrews encouragingly.

"To England," said Ernst.

The boys murmured and whistled in astonishment. Just then the bell rang. As the boys filed out of the room, Peter clapped Ernst on the shoulder, asking brightly:

"What did you do, fella? Stand in front of the microphone, and say: 'Is this Buckingham Palace'?"

Ernst smiled awkwardly and without answering, stepped into the washroom. Thursty followed him, but not for the usual water fight.

"Tell us about it, fella," he said interestedly.

"It was Mutti," said Ernst.

"Sure," said Thursty. He had a quick blurred image of Mutti, as she looked in the little old snapshot, standing in the sunshine beside Ernst's father, with the bicycle leaning against the side of the cottage. He wondered if Ernst had said anything about him.

"We couldn't speak to Pappi — to my father," said Ernst, wrinkling his forehead anxiously. "Some children spoke to both their parents."

"What children?"

"It was all arranged ahead by the BBC. Susi didn't tell us because she was afraid something would go wrong and then we would be so disappointed."

Ernst stopped. A couple of boys from another Form had come into the washroom, and were looking at him curiously as they splashed their hands in the basin. And he couldn't explain to Thursty what it had been like. The big room with all the microphones, and the boys and girls sitting about, as hushed as though they were in church, but inside, if they felt as he and Erica did, going hot and cold by turns. Most of them were about thirteen, but there were a few tiny ones. A little bit of a boy, about the size of Silly, wouldn't or couldn't speak at all. The minutes were running away, and the little boy hadn't said a word. One of the officials stood near, bending over him, trying to encourage him, but he was mute. And then suddenly he began to make a noise like a duck, and like a cat, and a dog, and a crowing rooster. And then he said, " 'By, Mummy!" and that was all. When it was Ernst's turn, he had to share the few minutes with Erica. Mutti's voice sounded clear and wonderfully close. She was all right, and Pappi, she said, choking a little, was safe, quite safe. But he couldn't speak to them. There seemed strangely to be plenty of time, but it was hard to know what to choose, of all the hundred things to say, and Mutti wanted them to do most of the talking. And all of a sudden it was over. And she was three thousand miles away.

"Jeepers creepers, the second bell!" cried Thursty.

In the rush for the next class he forgot all about Ernst's broadcast. He even forgot the plaguy assignment to write up his holiday. Thursty always preferred to draw pictures of things rather than write about them. It was too hard to find words, and besides, there was the question of spelling.

At last classes were over, and he was out on the field in his football togs. This was the hour for which he'd been waiting. He was keyed up by the fact that there were fellows from the higher Forms watching, and the coach had dropped a significant word about picking candidates for next year's Varsity. Thursty was to play halfback.

Jim Clark had given them an earful about the plays he'd seen in the Bowl. They finally persuaded the coach to let them try one, they called it the T-play. It was a new trick, and Thursty was a bit anxious as to how it would go. At the end of the first half they hadn't yet used it. Things hadn't gone too badly. Once Ernst had fumbled the ball, and another time he mistook the signal and tried to make the wrong play. But when the whistle blew, the score was 2:0 in their favor, no thanks to Ernie, as Jim Clark reminded him coldly.

The other team opened up with a touchback. Before long the score was reversed in *their* favor. Thursty, on his toes, wondered how soon Jim would give the signal for the T-play. They might get away with it, if only Ernst woke up. And Richy wasn't up to form, either.

The other team had the ball. They were waiting for the word from their quarterback. Suddenly things began to happen. The OTHER team was using the T-play! It was plain from the way they were running interference. Thursty dashed for the man with the ball. He made a swift pass. But the man who caught the ball fumbled it. Booker snatched it up. He was running with it. He was up against trouble. Swiftly he made a pass in turn. The darn fool! He had thrown it to Ernst!

There were too many thighs and shoulders in the way. Thursty couldn't see what was happening. He was prickly with sweat, his legs felt as though they had been pulled like the nose of the elephant's child, his chest was sore from running, and he heard, dimly, as from a distance, the yells of the onlookers. It seemed an eternity before he fought his way free and saw Ernst running, running with the ball tight in his arms. He was across the goal line. It was a touchdown. Before the advantage could be taken from them, the whistle blew for the end of the game.

The fellows from the Varsity were cheering. Even Pete was enthusiastic. Jim Clark all but apologized for having cracked down on Ernst so hard earlier. When the coach slapped Ernst on the back with the wordless wink that he reserved for special occasions, Thursty felt almost as good as if he'd won the game himself. Ernst mopped his flushed face, and grinned. He felt good, too.

In the damp clubbiness of the dressing room, they rehearsed the game, play by play.

"I only saw the end," Thursty shouted above the noise, before he had quite tuned down his shower. "You were a whiz, kid," he yelled, sticking his head out of the curtains.

Hastily they pulled and pushed themselves into their clothes — Thursty never bothered to towel himself dry enough to get his socks on easily — and tramped outside.

"You were a whiz," Thursty repeated, flinging an arm about Ernst's shoulders, as they came out on the school steps. "How'd you ever do it?"

Ernst smiled.

"Let's celebrate," said Thursty in a burst of generosity. "Come on down to the Soda Shoppe and have a coke on me."

"No, thank you, Thursty."

Ernst was running, with the
ball tight in his arms

Thursty was not surprised at the refusal. But there was something queer about the tone in which it was made. Withdrawing his arm, Thursty faced his friend.

"What's the matter?" he asked. "What's eating you?"

"Nossing." The telltale lisp made Thursty certain that something was wrong. He pulled Ernst down to a seat beside him at the bottom of the steps.

"Come on," he said. "Give!"

Just then Mr. Andrews, swinging his brief case, his hatless hair blowing, though the day was unusually mild for November, came out and ran down the steps toward them.

"Aren't you fellows kind of late?" Mr. Andrews asked. "There ought to be a better way than this of celebrating a touchdown."

So even Mr. Andrews had heard about it.

"That's what I call something to write home about," he said, adding quickly: "You can write to your mother, now she's in England."

"And my father," said Ernst, jealous for Pappi.

Mr. Andrews let that pass.

"You'll have something to tell Erica when you see her tomorrow, at any rate," he said. "So long!" And with an extra swing of his brief case, he turned and started walking down the hill.

Ernst got up from the step where he had been sitting, as if to follow.

"Wait a minute," said Thursty, getting up too. "You never told me what you were sore about."

Ernst did not answer at once, and Thursty prodded him.

"It's nothing to do with Andrews, is it?"

Ernst reddened, and shook his head.

"No," he said, and paused. "Tomorrow I go to Erica."

"Swell," said Thursty. But seeing Ernst's face as he stood there, fiddling with a loose button on the sleeve of his windbreaker, Thursty asked: "Or maybe it isn't? You don't mean — you're not going there to stay?"

Ernst nodded, with a queer little smile.

Gradually the story came out. Mutti — who had had no news of them for ever so long — had been quite sure that the twins were together with Aunt Frances and Uncle Stephen. Somehow they hadn't been able to tell her in those crowded minutes on the telephone what had happened. Aunt Frances and Uncle Stephen, who had heard the messages broadcast, were a little ashamed of themselves for the way they had behaved. They wanted to make up for it, now, at once.

And it wasn't as if Susi were trying to keep Ernst with her.

It would be much easier for Susi if he were gone. Then she could use the small room on the passage next to hers as it was needed. She had had to put the little Marguerite into her own room after the fire, until the child was well enough to go to her parents' new lodgings. With Ernst's room free, there would be a place to tuck a little girl who had been turned out, or a boy who suddenly developed a sore throat. As a matter of fact, there was an immediate emergency.

A few days before Thanksgiving a boatload of refugees had arrived, with a large quota of children. Some of them had found their way to The Welcome already. There would be more. That was fine, but among the new arrivals were a couple of small ones, stranded, as Ernst had been when there was no one prepared to receive him. Susi was taking these orphaned children, as she had taken him. She would have managed to squeeze them in somehow, under any circumstances. But this empty room lightened the burden. And it gave Tante Tilda less excuse for grumbling.

"I told you, Thursty," Ernst wound up, "it was nossing."

"Yeah," said Thursty, unconvinced.

Because, even after Ernst had explained everything, there were the things he hadn't said. He was going to live with Erica again, but he was also going to live with people who hadn't, at first, wanted him. And he probably wouldn't get to The Welcome much any more. Aunt Frances wouldn't understand his wanting to be there. And when he did go, it would be different. The Welcome wouldn't be home to him any more, with Susi at the center of it. Susi would be there, of course, but not in quite the same way. Susi had more people than just Ernst to think about. For instance: Mr. Andrews.

"What you grinning about, Thursty?" asked Ernst.

Thursty suppressed the grin. He felt that Ernst wouldn't like to think about Susi and Mr. Andrews. With Mutti off in England, Susi was the nearest thing to a mother that Ernst had. Mr. Andrews didn't fit into that picture.

"It'll be great," said Thursty hastily, "you and Erica being together again."

"Yes," Ernst answered, "great. Goodby, Thursty." And he turned off down the hill.

"Good-by," Thursty called after him.

As Ernst strode off in the gathering dusk and chill, Thursty had an odd sense of loneliness. He was glad when he saw his own house in the distance, and, nearing it, noticed a light in the cellar and imagined Pop at work on Silly's doll house. That sight cheered him further. After Thanksgiving, the next holiday was Christmas. He wondered what surprise Pop was going to spring on *him*.

CHAPTER SEVENTEEN

"Twinkle, twinkle, little star,
Who the heck do you think you are —
A flashlight?"

Thursty, astride a ladder in the art room, was chanting and painting at the same time. When Thursty painted, especially if he had a ticklish job like this, with only scanty gold paint for the stars and that likely to run into the blue wash of sky, he stuck his tongue out while he worked. What with chanting, and stopping to stick out his tongue reflectively, and then chanting again, the effect was something like this: "Twink" (pause for tongue business), "ul, twinkul, lit" (pause) "tul star!" (Pause.) "Who the heck" (pause) "do you think you" (long pause, then explosively) "ARE! A flashlight?"

He glanced at the clock. Ernst should be coming soon to help him with the job. He dipped his brush again carefully, and changed his chant to "Si-i-lent night, ho-o-ly night."

Ernst sang that song differently. In fact, he insisted that the right words were *"Stille Nacht, heilige Nacht."* Pete said he was darned if he was going to sing German. Ernst reminded him that the theme of this year's festival was "Christmas Everywhere." Pete only laughed. Thursty sided with Pete, simply because he didn't want to be bothered learning the foreign words. But he was pleased with Ernie.

It was nervy of him to have stood up to Pete the way he did. A couple of weeks ago he wouldn't have dared.

Ernie had changed. He was being talked about as possible Varsity material next year, and that had done something to him. Besides, the fellows considered him more of a regular guy since he had become part of a real family, even if it was only an adoptive one. He was living with Erica now, and Aunt Frances and Uncle Stephen were trying hard to make it up to him for not having accepted him right away.

Thursty, his head on one side, his brush poised, considered these things while admiring the last star he had painted in.

"When — in that — dim manger's light," he continued happily, and paused, conscious that someone had come into the room.

"Hello, Ernie, that you?" he asked, without turning round.

"No, it's not."

Thursty glanced down, then, to find Pete, a sheaf of papers in his fist, eyeing him militantly.

"What's up?"

"It's all right for you," said Pete in a sulky voice, "painting stars. Stars are the same all over."

"What do you mean?" Thursty looked from Pete to his shining scene, annoyed by this cavalier treatment of his handiwork.

"I mean," said Pete, "Andrews says we got to write a play about Christmas Everywhere. And here it's three weeks from the big day and it looks like Christmas Nowhere! Besides, it's a gyp. He told us this year we were going to concentrate on America, remember? And then he makes me write a

"Hello, Ernie, that you?" he asked,
without turning around

scene about *beau Noël*. What's American about *beau Noël?*"

Thursty might have agreed, but he was disgruntled because Pete had slighted his stars.

"Well," he said judiciously, "you know what Andrews said when he handed us the idea: Americans come from pretty much everywhere; the only natives are the Indians. You want a Redskin Christmas?"

"Oh, nuts!" cried Pete. "He says my scene's no good and I got to do it over. And he says if I can't get the stuff out of books, maybe there's some other way."

"Can't get any help from me, fella."

"I wasn't asking you," Peter corrected him. "I came to find Ernst."

"He's not a Frenchy."

"No, but he might have some dope on it anyway. He was in Paris once."

They were interrupted by the bell.

"I got to go," said Pete. "I got a committee meeting."

Thursty returned to his work. He hadn't been at it long when the door opened again, to admit Ernst.

"Pete was in here a minute ago looking for you," said Thursty. "He thought you could help him with this scene he's got to write."

Ernst didn't answer at once, and Thursty glanced around at him. He looked very queer. His face was pale and blotchy, like Silly's after she'd been crying.

"Say, fella," said Thursty, eyeing him, "were they testing the make-up on you?"

"No," Ernst replied in a subdued voice, adding quickly: "Don't you need some help?"

"I sure do," said Thursty, climbing down. "There's the other part of the sky to paint in. My arm's tired. How d'you like it?" And he stepped back to get a good view of his masterpiece.

"It's very good," said Ernst in the same low tone, and as though it didn't really matter. At the same time he moved the ladder into position so that he could get at the next strip to be painted.

"Golly, my arm's tired," Thursty repeated. "Wait till you start up there, you bet you'll think it's good then!"

Ernst climbed up and started painting in silence.

"Well," said Thursty, disappointed at getting no praise from this quarter either, "be seeing you," and banging the door behind him, he left Ernst alone.

Automatically he made for the gym. It was a not unexciting place at the moment. Off in one corner, grouped about the piano, the glee club was singing valiantly against the noise of hammering from the stage. At the other end of the gym Booker and Jim Clark were playing with a medicine ball. The floor was strewn with oddments of costume and properties, including a cracked pasteboard boar's head for the Old England scene and a portable radio for the modern South Pole one. Mr. Andrews, ruffling his hair, stood reading an inky page, while Richy, whose brain child it was, looked on in resigned despair. As Thursty came along, Mr. Andrews handed the sheet back to Richy with a shake of the head.

At once the other boys flocked about him.

"Mr. Andrews, they're trying to give me the wrong cue. Those lines were cut."

"When is the first dress rehearsal, Mr. Andrews? Because

my mother says if she has to finish my costume by Friday —"

"Oh, Mr. Andrews!"

It looked as though a rehearsal were about to start. Thursty edged nearer the better to see.

"Hello," said Mr. Andrews, noticing him. "Have you seen Ernst?"

"He's up in the art room, painting a backdrop," replied Thursty.

"Is he all right?"

"Yes, I guess so. That is —" Thursty stumbled over the answer, recalling Ernst's queer look and odd behavior.

"Here," said Mr. Andrews, suddenly thrusting the script into the hands of Jim Clark. "You carry on for me. It doesn't matter if they ad lib a bit, but see that they get the main cues. Come out here a minute, Thursty, I want to see you."

Thursty followed Mr. Andrews into the corridor, wondering.

"See here, Thursty, oughtn't you be up in the art room with Ernst?"

"Oh, golly, Mr. Andrews, my arm got awful tired. And besides, I wanted to ask you —" he stopped. Mr. Andrews didn't seem to be listening.

"It's not going to be a very jolly Christmas for Ernst," he was saying slowly, "or for Erica."

"They're not going to be separated again?" exclaimed Thursty.

"No, they're together for keeps, I guess. But —" Mr. Andrews glanced sharply at Thursty. "Didn't he tell you?"

Thursty shook his head.

"I think you ought to know," said Mr. Andrews. "There

isn't anybody at school who counts with Ernst the way you do, Thursty." He paused.

Thursty was pleased by this unexpected tribute, but there was more than a hint of trouble in Mr. Andrews' manner. He just stood there, running his fingers through his hair, and staring at the floor.

"I think you ought to know," he repeated. "They got bad news this morning about their father. You remember on the telephone their mother said he was safe." He paused again, and Thursty nodded dumbly.

"Well, he's safe enough. He died in the prison camp. She couldn't bring herself to tell them."

Thursty felt miserable. It wasn't so much sadness, because he couldn't take it in. It was mostly that he wouldn't know how to face Ernie, or what to say to him when he saw him again.

"Ernst's had a pretty tough time," said Mr. Andrews, slowly. "And you kids didn't make it any easier for him. At first, anyway. What was wrong, Thursty, do you know?"

Thursty fumbled for an answer. They *had* been mean to Ernie at the start, nobody knew it better than he did.

"Oh," he answered, looking at the floor, "he was such a — such a queer guy. He talked queer. And he didn't know anything. At least, not what he ought to have known."

Thursty stopped. It was hard to put into words, but the other fellows would have understood what he meant. They'd felt the same way about Ernst.

"I know," said Mr. Andrews, not unkindly. "Ernst didn't belong." He paused a moment before he went on. "It's a funny thing, Thursty," he said, "but you know that the word the old Greeks had for a foreigner was 'barbaros': that's what we get our word 'barbarian' from. But really, it's we who behave like barbarians when a stranger comes along." Mr. Andrews ruffled his hair as he always did when he was troubled or excited. He seemed not really to be aware of Thursty standing there uncomfortably beside him. It was almost as though he were talking to himself.

"Gosh," he said, "it makes me hot under the collar when I think about it. You kids, you weren't any blinder than a whole bunch of grownups who don't know that the thing that's worth while about people is just what makes them different. The ones who want everybody to be like everybody else never really looked at the world. When you think of all the shapes and colors and kinds of things there are, from the polar wastes to the African jungles, when you look at the planetary systems and remember the creatures you can't see with the naked eye, and then you see fellows insisting that everybody must be their very own kind, or else — Why, it's as though there were a Redheaded League or a Society of Hunchbacks who refused to play along unless everybody on earth dyed their hair red or wore a hump. I'm sorry, Thursty," — Mr. Andrews dropped his hand on Thursty's shoulder — "I shouldn't have let it out on you. But you see what I mean? It doesn't matter if you have red hair or black, if you're humped or straight: you've got to be yourself and let the other fellow be himself. That's why Ernie's father had to die: because there are people who want everything their own way and everyone to toe the line they've drawn. It's a rotten shame, and it means tough going for the rest of us for I don't know how long. And if we think we're not partly to blame, it'll be worse all around. But we'll make it. We've got to!

"About Ernst," Mr. Andrews began again, in a gentler voice.

"Ernie'll be all right," said Thursty, but without conviction. Sure, the boys liked him now. But that couldn't make up for what had happened to his father.

Suddenly Mr. Andrews pulled out his watch, frowned at it, and said hurriedly:

"Come on, Thursty. I've got to see those kids before they break up."

But Thursty didn't go back into the gym. He made for the locker room instead. He knew now why Ernie had looked so odd and been so uncommunicative when he came into the art room, why he hadn't admired Thursty's glittering stars. And again Thursty was suddenly reminded of the funny little snapshot with the two people blinking in the sunlight. It flashed upon him that he had never had a chance to make that enlargement of it he'd planned. But Ernst's Uncle Stephen could do it all right: he had better equipment than the whole Camera Club put together. But Ernst's Uncle Stephen probably didn't know that the snapshot existed.

He stood in front of his open locker, ages away from the hour when he'd been perched on the ladder, painting and singing. Awkwardly he shouldered into his lumberjacket and took hold of the zipper. As though to symbolize in little his sense of being brought up short by unmanageable facts, the zipper stuck and refused to move up or down.

"Hello, Thursty."

It was Ernst. Thursty looked up and reddened, embarrassed by the realization that Ernst's trouble was deeper than any he had ever known.

"Hello," he said. And then hurriedly, to cover his unease, "I can't make this darn thing budge."

"Let me try."

"Is the backdrop finished?" asked Thursty, just to say something, as Ernst began tugging.

Ernst nodded.

"Golly, it looks as though we'd have all the scenery and everything but the play," said Thursty. "Look out," he exclaimed, "you'll break it!"

"No," said Ernst quietly, with a final clever wrench, "it's O. K."

"Swell."

But as they marched out of the locker room into the frosty twilight, Thursty continued to frown. He wanted to tell Ernst that he knew, and yet he didn't want to talk about it. He parted from Ernst without having said anything. But he gave his friend's arm a specially hard squeeze in farewell. Then, glumly, he made for home.

He was so silent during dinner that Moth' thought he wasn't well. But Pop managed to get her off the subject, and when the pair of them went down cellar afterwards to work at Silly's doll house, life took on a more cheerful color. Thursty was putting some blue trim on the windows when he heard Moth' calling him to the telephone.

Who would be phoning me? Thursty asked himself, pleased at the summons. There was always a feeling of expectancy in answering the phone, just as there was in opening a letter, though the letter might be only an advertisement of a new breakfast cereal, and the message a request for the math homework from an absent classmate.

"Hello," said Thursty hopefully, "this is me."

"This is Pete. I want to ask you something."

"Yop," said Thursty.

"I got hold of Ernst all right. I saw him in the subway going home. I tried to pump him, but he didn't know a thing about *Noël*."

"Nope," said Thursty.

"But then, I don't know how come, all of a sudden he began telling me about his old hangout. You know: the Whozzis, the Hi-ya."

"Susi's," said Thursty. "The Welcome." He had to laugh, but at the same time he had an uncomfortable feeling that perhaps Peter was calling him because he wanted help in planning a fresh attack on Ernst.

"Listen, Pete," he began.

"You listen first," Peter interrupted. "According to Ernst, there's a kid at that place named Marguerite who knows all about *Noël*."

"That's right."

"Yes, and a fellow from Warsaw who could give Richy pointers on the Polish scene he's got to write. Ernst said there were kids from just about everywhere: Spaniards and Dutchies and all, including the Scandinavian."

"I know." A light was beginning to dawn on Thursty.

"That's why I'm calling you," said Pete. "I could of asked Andrews. He knows all about it. He does shopwork with the kids there Saturdays. But I couldn't get the straight dope from him, because he's only a teacher, and besides he's sold on the place. That's why I'm asking you. You ought to be able to tell me. Is it O.K. or is it wacky?"

"It's wacky," said Thursty, remembering the bewildered children and their scarcely less bewildered parents, the clamor of strange languages, the wild bomb game that the children played, the witchlike Tante Tilda. "But it's O.K.," he added, seeing Susi's warm cheek dimpling in a smile, Susi's golden-green eyes as she said quietly, *"Na,* that's all right."

"Thanks," said Pete. "That's all I wanted to know. 'By." And he hung up.

Slowly Thursty put the receiver back on the hook. Pete hadn't been very explicit, but Thursty understood that he was planning to draw upon the resources of The Welcome. And why not? Andrews had said more than once that they shouldn't get all their material out of books. I bet, Thursty said to himself shrewdly, this is what he wanted to have happen all along!

"Dwight Thurston, Junior!" It was Moth' again, wanting to know if he had finished phoning and reminding him that it was half an hour past bedtime.

"And do try to get some of that paint off your hair. It's Christmas festival everywhere with you," she joked.

Thursty grinned, and then he suddenly remembered Ernst's trouble, and Erica's, and felt lonesome and strange. But Aunt Frances and Uncle Stephen were turning out pretty decent, Thursty reflected. And there was always Susi. The thought of Susi brought up again the possibility Peter had intimated, of a get-together down at The Welcome.

It was with very mixed feelings indeed that Thursty made for the bathroom. Of course, he wasn't going to try to get the paint off his hair: that would have to wear off, or maybe, before dress rehearsal, he'd even have to have a haircut.

CHAPTER EIGHTEEN

The next morning Thursty got to school early. So did Pete. And Richy and Booker and Jim Clark and Ernst. It didn't take long for Pete to explain his idea to the others.

"Aren't most of the kids down there too young to be any use to us?" asked Jim, whose voice, perhaps because it had already changed, counted heavily.

"There are plenty of fellows there our age," said Thursty, "look at Ernie."

"Yes," Richy objected, "but half of those kids are girls. What good would they be?"

"Some girls aren't so bad," said Thursty, thinking of Erica.

"Besides," said Pete, "it isn't as if they were going to be in our festival, any of them. They're just going to tell us what to put in the scenes that we're stuck with. We don't really know about Christmas anywhere but here."

"And in Old England," put in Jim Clark, who had played the lord of the castle bidding his servitors bring in the Yule log too often to forget it.

"Looks to me," said Booker cheerfully, "like we're bound to get some new notions down there. Funny thing," he added, "my Uncle Bill, the one that was with the circus like I told you, he said everybody in the show had a foreign name. There was a fellow from Kansas called himself Don Alphonso, and the bareback rider, she came from Brooklyn I think, she was Mademoiselle Something or other. Even if we don't learn anything at The Welcome but some fancy names to use, it ought to help some."

"Ladislaus is fancy," said Richy hopefully.

Just then Mr. Andrews came into the room, whistling as though the festival weren't a recurrent headache. Thursty nudged Pete. They were bound to have Andrews on their side. But when Pete had explained the idea to him, he just hummed a little to himself and said,

"Well, what do you fellows think of it?"

"It's O.K.," said Thursty.

"Might work," Jim admitted.

"I think it is good," said Ernst. "Susi will like it, too."

"If Susi likes it," said Mr. Andrews, "why then . . ." But he didn't finish the sentence. He got rather red and began running his fingers through his hair.

If Susi likes it, thought Thursty with a private grin, you're all for it!

The rest of the class began coming into the room then, and pretty soon the first bell rang. It was clear to Thursty, however, that the matter was settled.

That was Friday. On Saturday a committee of inquiry composed of Pete and Thursty, Richy and Ernst, met at The Welcome.

Pete was annoyed to find, as Jim had warned them, a number of small children as useless as Silly, only worse because some of them didn't speak English. And there were also girls, including Erica. Thursty didn't know quite how to greet her: it was the first time he had seen her since her father died. But luckily Susi was there when they met, and she made it all right. The Polish boy called Ladislaus was not there. But there was another boy from the neighborhood of Warsaw who, though he had only the commonplace name of John, would be able to give Richy all the information he needed.

"It's got to be good!" exclaimed Susi. "Do you know what Mr. Andrews told me?" her warmly colored face dimpling happily. "He said our boys and girls who work with you, they will be invited to the dress rehearsal. *Na,* we must make it good!"

She was eager to help and had all the time in the world to give them. The only trouble was that other people kept interrupting. Tante Tilda came out to ask if the committee were staying to lunch.

"Why, of course!" said Susi.

At which Tante Tilda began muttering under her breath.

"If you do not have enough food . . ." began Susi. There was a twinkle in her eyes.

"Ach, Susi, you are not ashamed to say such a thing!" cried Tante Tilda angrily. "It is only that the grocer is late again." And she went off, shaking her gray head.

Susi laughed.

"You will see: she will make us an extra good lunch today just because she seems so cross."

She was about to return to the question of the festival when a howl went up from the room that served as a nursery. The mother of one of the littlest children had come home from work unexpectedly before noon, and was calling for her. But the child refused to leave. It took all of Susi's persuasive powers to get her out.

And then there was Mr. Andrews. Instead of staying

down below in the shop where he belonged, he kept coming up to consult with Susi about mysteries that took her away from everyone.

The queerest part of the day for Thursty was the half hour he spent with a new boy named David, who had come all the way from Palestine. David had never celebrated Christmas in his life. Thursty was so amazed at this that he hardly heard what David had to say about the Jewish feast of Hanukkah which fell just at Christmastime. He did gather, though, that it had a kind of Christmasy flavor. If there wasn't a tree with a Star on it, there were Hanukkah candles that had something to do with a legend of miraculous lights. And it meant lots of good things to eat and an exchange of presents, too.

"I never thought of it before," said David in a surprised voice, "but I suppose Jesus must have celebrated Hanukkah when he was our age: he was brought up as a good Jew. Maybe it was like a birthday party for him."

It almost made Thursty feel like trying to introduce a Hanukkah scene into the festival.

And finally, rather late, because of the tardy grocer, they were summoned to lunch. Just as Susi had prophesied, Tante Tilda had prepared something tasty, giving the committee sausage and pancakes to make up for the vegetables, and there was chocolate milk instead of the everyday kind, and Eskimo pie for dessert. They got red straws with the milk, which, though babyish, were rather jolly, especially when you got to the bottom of the glass and made funny noises with them. And there were lollipops afterwards.

Thursty went home at the end of the day feeling that the

festival might be a success, after all. It would certainly be different from anything they had ever done.

And then, so suddenly that he didn't know how the days had flown by, they were on the eve of the first dress rehearsal. Thursty was now convinced that the festival would be a flop. Susi's kids hadn't proven as helpful as they promised to be at first. They had been more interested in learning all about a real American Christmas than in talking of the celebrations that they had known in Europe. And every once in a while, just when you thought you were going to find out something truly exciting from them, they would say, "But the rest I forget."

Besides, nobody seemed to know his lines. Aside from the scenery, the only good thing, as far as Thursty could see, were the costumes. There was never anything quite like Pete got up as a French peasant or Richy as a Polish lord. Susi's kids had helped a lot there, not only with suggestions, but with surprising scraps from their parents' trunks. Thursty would have loved to take pictures of the boys in all their gaudy trappings, but his kodak seemed gone forever, and somehow he didn't feel like borrowing one. It wouldn't be quite the same.

To make matters worse, Mr. Andrews never seemed to be around when he was wanted. And he looked so pale and worn and was generally so cross that Thursty began to feel as Moth' did when Silly misbehaved, that maybe he was "coming down with something." There were moments, as during the first dress rehearsal, when Thursty rather hoped he was, because then they'd all be put in quarantine, and wouldn't have to give the play at all.

After a particularly bad performance, they were practicing the songs, most of which were foreign ones and quite new to them. They were to wind up with a favorite of Thursty's, a Ukrainian folk song, the English words of which were short and sweet:

Yuletide wakes, Yuletide breaks,
Woman, give me eggs and cakes.
If the cakes you do not give,
Your old ox will never live;
I will take him to the wood,
And will twist his horns for good.
If you make me stand and wait,
I will take away your gate.
If you will not give me eggs,
I will break your chickens' legs.
Yuletide wakes, Yuletide breaks,
Woman, give me eggs and cakes!

Thursty, tired and bored, decided to get some fun out of this at least. He cast his eyes about, so that the boys would know they were to follow his lead. Then he began, in as low a voice as he could manage:

"Yuletide wakes, Yuletide breaks," continuing in a beggar's slow whine: "Woman, give me eggs and cakes!"

"What sort of song do you think this is?" Mr. Andrews interrupted sharply. " 'Hallelujah, I'm a bum'? Start over again. And put some spirit into it!"

Thursty chuckled. This time he began singing very softly, and got noisier and noisier as he went on, until he threatened the chickens' legs with a shout. The others took their cue from him. The last lines sounded like a riot transmitted by loud-speaker.

"Is that what you call spirit?" demanded Mr. Andrews.

"Well, there's not much Christmas spirit in the song," said Thursty, sputtering with laughter.

Angry as he was, Mr. Andrews grinned briefly.

"Don't worry about that," he said. "Jim Clark will take care of that end of it." Jim Clark was to come in at the close of the performance as Father Christmas. "But see here," he said savagely, "do you fellows realize how soon the festival comes off? Maybe you don't give a hoot about making a good showing before the school" (oh, but they did, and he knew it), "still you don't want to let certain other people down." (Did he mean Susi's kids?) "They don't come up for the games. Your report cards aren't much more than scraps of paper to them." (No, not Susi's kids.) "The festival is the one chance your fathers and mothers have to see what you can do when you've put all you've got into it. By the way," he added, in a tone of deep irony, "I don't suppose you ever get anything from your parents. Hands up, those of you who are so rash as to expect something from them when Christmas comes round." He smiled at them sardonically. And then, as Mr. Andrews looked at the raised hands, his face twisted in an expression of almost physical pain, and he looked away.

"All right!" he said harshly, as he faced them again. "We'll go over this tomorrow at nine sharp. You're dismissed."

"The bell hasn't even rung yet," Thursty said in a puzzled whisper, turning to his neighbor. It was Ernst.

With a kind of backward vision Thursty recalled that when every other boy had his hand up, and some of them both hands, Ernst hadn't raised his at all. He didn't expect anything from a father who was dead and a mother three thousand miles way. And Mr. Andrews knew it. And hated himself for having mentioned fathers and mothers. That was why he had shouted at them and let them go.

And then without warning, it seemed, the evening of the final dress rehearsal was upon them. And the kids from The Welcome were coming to see it. And so were their own fathers and mothers (the school saw the performance the following afternoon). It was really like a first night. Horribly exciting. And, Thursty thought, sure to go wrong.

He peeked through the hole in the curtain. There were Pop and Moth', on the left side down near the front. And Granny was with them, too. And beside her the Armands, with the little Marguerite. Yes, and even Silly! They were letting her stay up late for the occasion. Thursty wished they hadn't. Not that he grudged Silly her small pleasures, but because at the last moment, Jim Clark having sprained his ankle, the part of Father Christmas had been turned over to Thursty. He had stage fright already. He had had no time to learn it properly. He was bound to stumble. He couldn't bear to make a fool of himself before Silly.

"There's Erica," whispered Ernst, who had followed him at the curtain hole. That made Thursty feel worse. "And Aunt Frances."

"And your Uncle Stephen?" asked Thursty, not that he cared about one person more or less, but just to keep from thinking about how it would feel with all of them looking

Ernst hadn't raised his hand at all

at him and listening to him, and he unable to utter a syllable.

"Uncle Stephen is backstage," said Ernst.

"Why?" asked Thursty, surprised.

"He's going to take pictures of us."

And again, curiously, Thursty recalled the funny little old snapshot. He had never done anything about it.

Turning abruptly, he almost bumped into Uncle Stephen, armed with one of his magnificent cameras, consulting with Mr. Andrews. Mr. Andrews had been unexpectedly jolly this evening and now was grinning broadly. As Thursty moved away he noticed that Uncle Stephen was pumping Mr. Andrews' hand in a congratulatory way.

And the play hadn't even started! He'd behave differently when it was all over, thought Thursty glumly.

"Hello, Thursty," said Uncle Stephen, giving Mr. Andrews a final clap on the shoulder. "Isn't it wonderful?"

Thursty looked at him blankly. And then he looked at the camera.

"*That's* wonderful," he said in a weak voice, partly because it seemed a silly thing to say, and partly because he couldn't dismiss the thought of what was going to happen during the final scene. And there was such an endless time to wait until then, too.

"It takes good pictures," responded Uncle Stephen. "And that reminds me, Thursty: did you ever get your kodak back, the one that was stolen? Ernst was telling me that sad story."

"Never," said Thursty. "Guess I never will, now."

"But our friend, M. Armand, I know his story, too — he would not sell you his?"

"He got a job soon after his little girl went to Susi's, and so he didn't have to sell his. He didn't want to, really," said Thursty.

"Hmmm, that's too bad," said Uncle Stephen, but absent-mindedly: he was setting his tripod in position. "I will take most shots from down front, but this side view isn't bad," he murmured to himself.

"Hi, Thursty!" It was Mr. Andrews again, calling him to the make-up room.

And all of a sudden Mr. Andrews was megaphoning a whispered "Lights out," the chorus began singing the opening measures of the song to which the curtains parted: "We three kings of Orient are," the lights in the gym went out, the footlights went on, and Booker, in the grand robes of one of the Three Kings, was stepping onto the stage. It had begun.

CHAPTER NINETEEN

Thursty, perspiring with dread and grease paint, stood watching, and listening for the familiar lines. It seemed to him that he knew by heart everybody's speech but his own. He had heard so many rehearsals, but for one reason or another, he had generally been off stage as Jim Clark pronounced the closing words. Booker was doing all right. The rest of the scene went off as it never had before. There was resounding applause from the audience as the curtains closed again, and then an appreciative murmur.

I bet, thought Thursty, it'll all be swell, and then the final scene will come and I'll go out there and not know my lines and spoil the whole thing. And indeed, it did go remarkably well. Only once Richy forgot his part and then Mr. Andrews prompted him so quickly and softly that nobody guessed. And the Give-me-eggs-and-cakes song made everybody laugh. And when the glee club sang "Silent Night," some of the audience joined in, and soon nearly everyone was singing. Uncle Stephen didn't sing: he was too busy with his camera, but he was very silent and efficient and nobody noticed him but Thursty, who wished with all his heart that he had nothing to do but take pictures of the performance. As a matter of fact, Uncle Stephen seemed to be all over the place. He even started to take a picture of the audience while some scene-shifting was going on.

Thursty couldn't see the point of that. The time to snap the audience was while they were looking at the stage. But then he saw that Uncle Stephen was focusing on Susi. She was standing in the aisle, looking up at Mr. Andrews, and he was looking down at her, with such complete concentration that you would have thought there was nobody else in the whole gym. They'll go into a clinch in a minute, thought Thursty. I guess it's settled, and that's why Andrews is so cocky.

"Got it," murmured Uncle Stephen with a chuckle, as Mr. Andrews squeezed Susi's arm and turned back to the wings.

Thursty, not wanting to be caught staring, turned too, and almost knocked down Ernst, who was standing right beside him, and must have seen just what he saw.

"Some picture!" he whispered, wondering if it could make any difference to Ernie now that he no longer lived with Susi.

"I was going to tell you," said Ernst. "Susi told us first," he added. "Tonight. Erica and me. You know, I think that was why Mr. Andrews was so cross: Susi took so long to say yes. She told us that she was afraid."

"Susi afraid?" asked Thursty incredulously.

"Only of things like going to the dentist, or getting married."

The scenery was in place now, and the boys retired. Thursty, no longer diverted by the thought of Susi, began to get nervous again. Soon he would have to go on. He didn't know anything about getting married, but this was worse than sitting in the dentist's waiting room. He felt as though a lot of little clocks were ticking away inside of him, his face was hot and his hands were cold. It was awful. He tried to go over his lines in his head, but the speeches of the others distracted him.

And then, with the whole cast assembled on the stage, the footlights blazing, the spot waiting to fix him, Thursty had finally to go on. He felt like somebody else in his gay red costume and his woolly white wig and beard, but it wasn't Father Christmas exactly, it was just a stranger.

The spotlight fell full on him. He scarcely saw the crowd behind and around him in their variegated costumes. It was dim out in front, so that he couldn't distinguish even the faces he knew. The distressing clockwork business inside him was no longer running. But there was a queer sensation in his throat, and a blurry view before him. And his brain seemed to have stopped. He couldn't remember a syllable of Jim Clark's speech. He could hear Mr. Andrews trying to prompt him, but he couldn't make out what the stage whisper meant.

He had to do something. He began speaking. They weren't the words he was supposed to say, and as he began with "Merry Christmas, everybody!" there was a slight titter from the wings. But he didn't care. He couldn't just stand there like a dumb ox, with Pop and Moth' and Silly and Susi and Erica, and the rest out there, expecting something from him. The heck with Jim Clark's speech! He'd have to "ad lib," as Mr. Andrews put it. He wetted his dry lips and began again.

"Merry Christmas," he repeated. "And, and thank you for being such a good audience." This time there was a little laugh from down in front. Thursty swallowed and went on hastily. "And thank you for helping us, some of you, you know who I mean, helped us a lot, showed us how Christmas could be celebrated different ways in different places. Because the important thing isn't whether you put the presents in a stocking or in a wooden shoe, it's the presents themselves that matter: giving somebody something. Like it doesn't matter either if you sing, 'Come All Ye Faithful' or '*Adeste Fideles*,' the words are different but they mean the same thing."

As he went on, Thursty felt a curious release, as though his own words didn't matter now because he had the attention of everybody and through his awkward phrases something significant that he felt at the moment dimly but unmistakably shone. At that moment Jim Clark's speech came back to him:

"I am Father Christmas," he began, "and here in my pack I carry what each of you wishes for most." But even as he spoke he forgot what followed. Not knowing what to say next, he repeated slowly: "What each of you wishes for most," and paused, and said, in a rounder voice than he had ever used: "Peace on earth, good will to men."

The curtains fell together. Out there in front they burst into thunderous applause. The boys crowded round Thursty, laughing and clapping his shoulder.

"That wasn't your speech, fella!"

"You got what I want most, Father Christmas?"

"You're O.K., Thursty!"

And then the curtains parted again, with the lights on, and Thursty, standing between Booker and Ernst, could see them down there clapping and smiling, and Erica was waving wildly — was it at him or at Ernst? And Silly was pointing and calling out in a shrill sweet voice: "That's my brother: Father Christmas is my brother!"

The spotlight fell on Thursty

And then he was down among them all, and Susi was saying:

"Congratulations, Thursty. You were wonderful!"

"I guess maybe I ought to say congratulations, too," muttered Thursty, hotter than ever with pleasure and embarrassment, pulling off his beard for relief.

"*Na*, how did you know?" asked Susi, dimpling.

Thursty grinned without answering. And suddenly, he didn't know how it happened, perhaps because he was so excited, he asked her the question that had been at the back of his mind all this time:

"But Susi, are you going to start a chicken farm?"

"My dear boy," Susi laughed, "with all those chicks of mine at The Welcome! And Bob's chicks at school — only of course they are bigger."

So that was all right. Bob must be Mr. Andrews. Thursty didn't even mind being called a chick. Besides, Susi understood that they were bigger.

"Hello," said Ernst, coming up.

"Oh, Ernst," said Erica, "you were fine! I didn't recognize you at first. And wasn't Thursty good?"

At which Thursty flushed again. And then Uncle Stephen appeared out of nowhere.

"I can't wait to develop them," he said to Aunt Frances.

"And we'll send them to Mutti," said Aunt Frances, with an arm about Erica and a quick smile for Ernst, "as soon as they're finished, so she won't be too surprised when she sees you."

"But —" said Thursty, astonished.

"And what a welcome she will get!" said Susi.

Ernst and Erica did not speak at all. They just looked at each other.

It was an hour afterward, when he was almost all dressed to go home, that Thursty, rubbing hopelessly at the grease paint and giving it up as a bad job, remembered one puzzling thing. Why had Uncle Stephen asked him that question about his kodak?

But he did not find out until Christmas morning.

9 -71